In the title
toy-themed
cation requ
eration.

Mistress Nora might be the one flogging the clients, but her sexy French boss, Kingsley, is the real sadist who rarely gives her a day off. They strike a backseat deal: Nora gets a month off in Europe if she can sneak into a rival kink club and get dirt on the owner. But she'll need more than her little red riding crop when she comes face-to-face with the club's dominant owner, Brad Wolfe...

Also included are five interlocking stories from the Original Sinners vaults—and one never-before-published story—featuring handcuffs, ropes, blindfolds, and other adult toys.

RELEASE DATE: SEPTEMBER 27, 2021
PUBLICITY: astoria@8thcircle.com
8th Circle Press / Dist. by Ingram
Mass-Market Paperback, 178 pp.
Retail: $12.95 US • ISBN: 978-1-949769418
eBook: $3.99 US • Audiobook: $TBD

THE ORIGINAL SINNERS
PULP LIBRARY

Vintage paperback-inspired editions of standalone novels and novellas from *USA Today* bestseller Tiffany Reisz's Original Sinners erotic romance series.

THE AUCTION

IMMERSED IN PLEASURE and

SUBMIT TO DESIRE

THE LAST GOOD KNIGHT

LITTLE RED RIDING CROP

MISCHIEF

THE MISTRESS FILES

LITTLE
RED
RIDING
CROP

LITTLE RED RIDING CROP

ADULT TOY STORIES

TIFFANY REISZ

8TH CIRCLE PRESS • LOUISVILLE, KY

"The Assistant" originally published in *Best Women's Erotica of the Year, Vol. 1.* "The Letter" originally published in *Serving Him.* "Little Red Riding Crop" originally published by Harlequin as a standalone ebook. "Movie Night" originally published in *Three of Hearts: Erotic Romance for Women.* "Rectified" originally published in *Baby Got Back.* "Tying the Knot" originally published in *Best Bondage Erotica 2013.*

All stories except "Little Red Riding Crop" and "The Chambermaid" originally edited by Rachel Kramer Bussel for Cleis Press.

Mass-Market Paperback ISBN: 9781949769418

Also available as an ebook and audiobook

Cover design by Andrew Shaffer. Front cover image used under license from Shutterstock.com. Interior images used under license from Shutterstock.com.

Second Edition / ADVANCE READING COPY

CONTENTS

LITTLE RED RIDING CROP

Rookies.

Nora rolled her eyes as she lifted her handcuffed wrists and pretended to scratch her ear. Most days she cursed her unruly black hair for its mass of waves and curls that took an hour to tame. But she loved it on days like these.

With a quick flick of her fingers, she removed a hair pin and surreptitiously bent it into the perfect shape. In less than five seconds she'd popped the handcuffs open just as Detective Cooper dropped into the chair behind his desk.

Flashing her dark green eyes at him, Nora threw her booted legs up onto his desk, crossed her feet at the ankles, and tossed the cuffs at him.

Cooper hadn't walked the beat in years,

but he still had his street reflexes. The wickedly handsome detective caught the cuffs with the tip of his fingers.

"Seriously, Nora." He held the handcuffs up. "Do you want to get locked up?"

She cocked her head to the side and smiled at him. "Isn't that the question I usually ask you, Coop?"

With a groan, Cooper rubbed his forehead. She'd never seen a black man blush so thoroughly before. Part of her wanted to crawl over his desk and kiss him just to make the public humiliation complete. A petite but stacked white dominatrix in red leather knee-high boots, a red and black mini-skirt with a matching corset crawling across the desk of a six-foot-tall tough-as-nails police detective and giving him a kiss on the tip of his nose? The temptation to out Detective Cooper as a secret male submissive nearly overwhelmed her. But she restrained herself. Number one, she liked Cooper and wouldn't do that to such a nice guy. And number two, she was a professional. No freebies for anyone.

"Nora…" He sat back in his chair and studied her with a mix of half-hearted disgust and barely disguised amusement. "You can't take off the cuffs yourself. It's considered re-sisting arrest."

"Then tell your damn rookies that when they arrest a professional dominatrix they might want to cuff her hands behind her back instead of in front."

"Would that have really stopped you?"

Nora thought about it a moment. "Prob-ably not. But it would have slowed me down. Can I go now?"

"In a hurry?"

"Places to go. People to beat. And you and I both know I didn't do anything wrong. S&M is not illegal in the state of New York."

Cooper opened a file nearly as tall as his coffee mug—her file. "The maid who stopped by the house to pick up her cell phone and heard 'gut-wrenching screams,' as she called them, would beg to differ."

"The maid wasn't paying to get the shit beat out of her. My client was. Only he can press charges, and he won't because he's scared of me. He pays extra to be scared of me. So I'm going, right? You're letting me go, aren't you? Say 'yes, Mistress.'"

Cooper sighed heavily.

"Coop...say it," Nora ordered.

"Fine. Yes, Mistress. You're free to go," he

said as Nora pulled her legs off the desk and started to stand up. "The boss man is outside waiting on you anyway."

She collapsed into the chair again.

"Cuffs, put them on me. Now. Slammer. Lock and key. Never let me out. Please please please, Coop. This is me begging you. Record it. You'll never hear it again."

"That bad, eh?"

Nora put on a pout, and sunk deeper into the chair. "He's going to yell at me."

Cooper rolled his dark eyes at her. "Nora...grow up. You're a dominatrix. Have some dignity."

"But he's got the sexy French accent and the whole 'I'm very disappointed in you' thing, and I just can't handle that right now."

Nora turned pleading eyes to the detective.

"Go. Out." He waved his hand at the door. "Scoot before you embarrass me even more."

With a growl, Nora rose out of the chair and glared down at Cooper giving him her best dominant stare.

"We still on for Thursday at eight?" she asked.

"Oh, hell yes." Cooper broke into a smile.

She grabbed her toy bag from the floor by

his desk and flung it over her shoulder. "Later, Coop. Don't do anything I wouldn't do."

"We figure out what that was yet?" he called out after her.

Nora hit the police station hallway. "Nope."

As soon as she walked outside a raindrop hit her forehead. Not wanting to ruin her leather she skipped nimbly down the front steps toward a silver stretch Rolls Royce idling in front of the station. A driver stepped out and opened the door for her. Throwing herself inside, Nora landed across the lap of a man reclining on the wide back seat.

The man raised his eyebrow and looked down at her as she pulled herself into a sitting position. Slowly the Rolls pulled away from the curb and still the man didn't speak. Fine, if he wanted a staring competition, he'd get a staring competition. Nora locked her eyes on his and waited. She could do this forever if she had to. After all, there weren't many men in New York, hell, even the world more fun to stare at than Kingsley Edge. Long dark hair held back tonight in a ponytail, deep brown eyes, olive skin...In his long military coat, embroidered vest, and riding boots he looked so damn handsome she wanted to slap him for it. But she refrained. Kingsley would like that too much.

"What?" she demanded when he still hadn't spoken after a whole thirty seconds of their staring contest.

"*Ma cherie*...I do not know what to do with you."

Even worse than being handsome, he had that fucking French accent she had to put up with.

"Do with me? I didn't do anything other than my job. Not my fault the maid overheard the ambassador screaming like a banshee."

"You broke the skin."

Nora shook her head and looked out the back window. Behind them she saw an SUV with a nice, normal-looking husband at the wheel and a perfectly plain wife pointing out something from the passenger seat. Their two-point-five kids probably sat in the backseat with little baggies of Cheerios and their crayons. Normal people, Nora told herself. Normal people did not have these kinds of conversations with their bosses.

She was so glad she wasn't normal people. "He tips better when you make him bleed."

"You went too far tonight," Kingsley said, crossing one long leg over the other. "I want to know why."

With reluctance Nora turned her eyes back to his. "I've just been...stressed. Guess I took it out on His Ambassadorness."

Kingsley reached out and rested his hand on her knee right where the top of her boot met her thigh. The feel of his fingers on her skin caused her to take a quick breath, a quick breath that Kingsley clearly heard.

"Stressed, *ma cherie*? Or frustrated?" He let his hand trail an inch higher up her leg.

"Frustrated," she confessed. "I work all the time, King. I don't have any time for...myself."

Nora's stomach tightened as Kingsley's low sensual laugh filled the back of the car. "How old are you?" he asked.

"You know how old I am."

"Answer me."

Nora exhaled noisily. "Thirty-one."

"Thirty-one years old...and the most beautiful woman in New York. There's no reason you should be sleeping alone."

"Other than the fact that a certain someone works me constantly so I can't get a single day off."

In a good week Nora could make ten to

fifteen thousand dollars off her rich and kinky clients. In two years Kingsley had turned her into the most in-demand domina-trix in America. Some clients flew in from across the country or even in from other countries for a few hours of her time. With Kingsley getting fifteen percent of every penny she made, he kept her dance card as full as possible. And she was starting to get sick of it.

"You exag—"

"I haven't had sex with someone other than myself in two months."

Kingsley's eyes widened in shock. If Kingsley went even two days without sex...no, pointless train of thought. Kingsley would never go two days without sex.

"Two months? *Quelle horreur, ma cherie.* Surely there's something I can do to make it up to you..."

"A day off would do. Or two. Or..."

"Or...?"

Kingsley brought his other hand between her knees and eased her thighs apart.

"King..." Nora said in a warning tone, a warning Kingsley didn't heed. He brought his mouth down and kissed her bare thigh.

Slowly he pushed her skirt higher with his mouth.

"I'm at your service, *Maîtresse*," he whispered against her skin.

Nora groaned at the back of her throat. Damn that man. All of New York's Underground considered Kingsley Edge their King of Kink. Sexy accent, handsome face, beautiful body, mysterious past...he was born to be the perfect dominant and would have been but for one small thing—secretly he was a switch.

Just like her.

"Your orders, *Maîtresse*?"

"Just keep doing that. I'll think of some orders in a minute or two."

He slipped her panties down her legs and Nora's thighs fell open.

"You don't let me do this with any of my clients," Nora reminded him as he parted her folds with his fingertips. He kissed her clitoris gently at first and then with greater force and hunger.

Kingsley paused for a moment to answer, "I hadn't planned on paying for this."

"Good. Because I'm out of your price range." She threaded her fingers through his hair and pushed his head back down. When

Kingsley laughed his rich French laugh into her, Nora gasped. One booted ankle landed on the back of the seat in the window. There. That would give Mr. and Mrs. SUV behind them something to talk about.

Nora clung to the leather interior as Kingsley pushed two fingers into her and found her g-spot. She clenched around his hand as her hips rose up. He worked all the magic his French tongue had on her. The muscles in her lower back tightened. The pressure built hard and high. After a few minutes of *the Kingsley Edge treatment*, she came with the force of two miserable months of celibacy behind her.

Panting, she lifted her head and watched Kingsley sit up and run the back of his hand over his wet lips. She wanted to kiss him, to taste herself, to thank him for the pleasure and the attention. But he was her boss. And she'd hardly thank the man for one orgasm when he was the reason she'd gone two months without.

"Lovely," Nora said as she pulled her leg out of the back window. "But that only makes up for about a week."

Kingsley gave her his best French pout.

"Fine. Two weeks then. But it'll take more

than a backseat..." Nora paused, realizing she of all people couldn't come up with the female equivalent of blowjob, decided to make one up, "a backseat v.j. to make up for two months of nothing."

Kingsley sighed as he sat back and adjusted his trousers. Clearly he was in the mood to knock out another week or two.

"Please..." Nora stared at him and let the mask of the infamous dominatrix fall off her face. "I'm tired, King. And I'm..." She couldn't quite get the word out. Kingsley had said "frustrated." The more accurate term would have been "lonely."

He studied her face in silence. He must have seen the truth in her words, in her eyes. She sensed his resistance give way.

"You are a dangerous woman, Nora Sutherlin. This is the last time I employ someone more manipulative than I."

"I learned from the best." She smiled at him, a shallow hollow smile that covered the loneliness they both felt for the one man who could twist them both around his perfect fingers. But she wouldn't think about him today. Or ever again.

Nora said nothing more as she watched

Kingsley wrestle with what little was left of his conscience.

"One month vacation."

Nora sagged in the seat. She could have cried with relief and kissed the French out of the man with gratitude but...

"But."

"But? I should have known there would be a but." Nora sat back up again and gave Kingsley's "but" the attention it deserved.

"But I need you to do an errand first. Complete the errand successfully, and I shall tell the Underground that your services have been engaged in Europe for the next month. I'll even send you to Europe, the country of your choice."

Nora raised her eyebrow. "What sort of errand is this?" To earn an entire month off plus a trip to Europe on Kingsley's dime, Nora knew she'd probably have to kill somebody. Two months without sex and she was about ready to.

"Black Forest. I need you to go there."

Nora's eyes widened. "Kingsley...that's—"

"They are more afraid of us than we are of them."

"Then why are you sending me instead of going yourself?"

Kingsley crossed his arms over his chest and threw his booted feet up on the seat by her thighs. His every move seemed designed to show how relaxed he was, how laid back. She didn't buy it.

"They would never let me in. I'm the enemy."

"And I work for you which also makes me the enemy," she reminded him.

"Black Forest is poaching my employees. They took Mistress Irina last month."

"I know but—"

"Hunt quit today."

Nora had heard about Irina, Kingsley's Russian dominatrix, defecting to Black Forest —the only BDSM club in Manhattan that could give Kingsley's Underground Empire a run for its money. That had hurt. But losing Hunt, the sexiest male submissive in all of New York and one of Kingsley many bedtime companions? That was personal.

"So I'm supposed to go there and what? Ask for Hunt back?"

"Black Forest is a mystery even to me," Kingsley said. "No one ever gets to meet *La Grande Dame*. She won't return my calls, answer my notes..."

"She's smart then." She'd heard of *La*

Grande Dame or just The Dame to the Underground. The Dame was something of a shadowy figure. Kingsley positioned himself as the King of the Underground, the face of Kink. He had no shame and lived so publicly he would have traded shares of his empire on the stock exchange had the businesses been legal. But The Dame had no face anyone had seen and no name Nora had ever heard. She couldn't be touched, couldn't be influenced, and most importantly, couldn't be seduced by Kingsley Edge.

"Too smart. I don't like not knowing my enemy. Go in if you can, find out something, anything for me. A name. A face. Or at the very least get her to stop stealing my people. Anything and you'll have your month off in Europe. If you can get Hunt back, you can take him with you."

"Now that is a serious offer." Nora knew she really didn't have anything to lose. If worse came to worse, they wouldn't let her in, she wouldn't get her month off, and life would go on as usual. No real danger involved except for failure. No real danger but for...but surely not. He wouldn't be there...would he? "Brad's not still there...is he?"

Kingsley didn't answer.

"Shit." Nora collapsed onto her side.

"One month, *cherie. Oui ou non?*"

Nora straightened up again. "Fine. Fine fine fine. *Oui.* I'm going. I'll go. Maybe Brad won't be there today. Am I going today?"

"You're going right now."

Kingsley nodded at the window. The Rolls Royce had pulled up to a dark alley shrouded by two overhanging trees. The trees had inspired the name of Black Forest. One didn't see big trees often in New York except in Central Park and yet these two seemingly had sprung from nowhere to serve as guardians of the club entrance.

As she gazed down the dark alley, water started to pound on the roof of the car as the rain turned to a storm.

"No. Today's not good. I can't get my leather wet."

Kingsley reached under the seat and pulled out a red cloak with a hood. "No more excuses."

With a growl, Nora grabbed the cloak and pulled it around her. She covered her hair with the hood and looked once more down the alley.

"If I don't make it back alive tell You-Know-Who—"

"You will be fine. Go. *Vite!*" Kingsley waved his hand.

Nora sighed. "You'll wait here for me, right?"

"*Bien sûr,*" Kingsley said.

Nodding, Nora opened the door and stepped into the rain. Just to be on the safe side, she brought her toy bag with her. The items in her toy bag were designed for inflicting pain—consensual pain, but pain nonetheless. If she was heading into Black Forest, she would go armed.

Staring down the dark alley, she steeled herself. She could do this. She had Kingsley as her backup in case anything...

From behind her she heard the sound of squealing tires. Kingsley had gone.

Nora could only roll her eyes. "Fucking Frenchman..." she mumbled as she strode forward. "It's like World War II all over again."

Early afternoon still, the club hadn't yet opened. The heels of her boots echoed hollowly off the wet concrete and the sound followed her to the green door at the entrance to Black Forest.

A rare case of nerves overtook Nora.

She'd beaten the shit out of some of the biggest, toughest men in the world if they paid her enough for the privilege. But they'd wanted her to, invited her to...Here at Black Forest, she came unwanted, uninvited. And Black Forest had the biggest damn dom in all of Manhattan. To comfort herself, she took her red riding crop out of her toy bag and held it by the handle. One never knew...

Nora tried the doorknob and found it locked. No worries there. She started to open her toy bag to dig out her lock-pick set when the door flew open so suddenly she gasped.

The man said nothing, asked no questions, and made no introductions. Of course, he didn't need to say anything or make any introductions. Nora knew Brad, had seen him before, had met him before...but no matter how many times she'd seen him she could never wrap her mind around the sheer size of the man. At six foot four he stood no taller than her tallest ex-lover. But where most tall men tended toward the lean side, Brad was muscle from shoulder to shoulder, neck to ankle, and so wickedly handsome with his lupine smile and his salt and pepper hair that Nora could never look at him without wanting to get hip to hip.

Enemy, she reminded herself sternly. No fraternizing with the enemy.

"Shouldn't you be at the gym?" Nora recovered her composure quickly. "I can see you shrinking by the second."

"Well..." he said looking Nora up and down. He seemed to take particular note of what she held in her hand and her red cloak. "If it isn't Little Red Riding Crop."

Nora gave him her brightest, broadest, most obnoxious smile. "If it isn't the Big Brad Wolfe. We meet again."

"And me not even properly dressed." Brad wore nothing but a pair of loose-fitting black pants and a black shirt...unbuttoned.

"I have that same shirt." Nora tapped her chin. "Well, actually it's a bed sheet. Same size. Very comfy."

"I've heard tales of your bed, Mistress. Urban legends."

"I live in Connecticut. They'd have to be suburban legends. I've heard tell of your bed too. Trees for bedposts, right?"

"You're getting me confused with Odysseus."

Nora raised an eyebrow, impressed despite herself. "Brawn and brains—I would never have guessed. But then again, I don't know anything about you."

"Born in Albany. Played football at Rutgers. Rhodes scholar. Love kink. Hate normal jobs. Divorced. No kids. There. That's the beginning and end of my life story."

"Divorced, huh? Vanilla ex-wife?"

"How'd you guess?"

"I'm smart too. Used to a fuck a Rhodes scholar. By the way...are you going to invite me in?"

"Should I?"

Nora thought about that question and decided honesty would win her more points than charm. "Nope."

Brad raised a dark eyebrow at her and said nothing. Maybe she should have gone with charm.

While waiting for Brad to make up his mind, Nora started to twirl her riding crop in her hand like a baton. She did that often when burning off nervous energy.

Brad merely watched her. How many staring contests with gorgeous men was she going to get into today?

"If I let you in, will you promise not to break anything...or anyone?" Nora spun the crop one more time.

"Nope."

"The Dame will have my hide if I let you in and you know it."

"Then let's hope you're into that sort of thing."

Nora smiled again at him, the smile she reserved for midnight conversations whispered across black sheets. It seemed to work. Brad took a step back and let her pass.

Finally inside Black Forest, Nora took a moment to simply look around. Kingsley's Underground Empire included half a dozen clubs all over Manhattan. But he only had one club that existed solely for their kind. The 8th Circle, as it was known to insiders, had been carved from the ruins of an old condemned hotel. Kingsley hadn't done much to spruce up the joint. The seediness of the club suited the clientele. But where The 8th Circle quietly catered to money, Black Forest reeked of it. Black chandeliers with black light bulbs swung low from the black and gold ceiling. Leather chairs and sofas littered the floor. A dozen doors lined the first and second levels —doors that led to private rooms for secret activities.

"You don't like it, do you?" Brad came to

stand behind her so close she could feel the heat of his skin radiating from his bare chest.

"Bit middle-class, isn't it? Got a Rotary Club feel to it."

"It's a helluva lot nicer than that shit-hole you work in."

"Exactly. We don't have to look pretty to get our millionaires through the door. They get that at home."

"Black Forest is doing extremely well."

"Must not be doing that well if you have to keep poaching Kingsley's people." Nora spun around and attempted to stare Brad down. It would have worked but she had to look too far up to stare him down.

"Kingsley works his people into the ground. No days off. No breaks. No vacations."

"He's a sadist."

"He's a bad boss."

"And The Dame is so much better?"

"She is actually."

"Then I should meet her," Nora said, heading toward the stairs. "We can talk 401Ks and dental insurance. You get dental, right?"

For a man built like a linebacker, Brad could move with shocking speed. He interposed himself between Nora and the staircase and stared down at her.

"That's not fair." Nora flashed him a frown. "If I can't stare you down you can't stare me down."

"You're on The Dame's territory. She makes the rules. I enforce them."

"Great plan. I'd like to talk to her about it." Nora tried to push her way past Brad and got nothing for her trouble but a few delicious seconds with her hand on his chest.

"No one talks to The Dame."

"Then I'll just listen."

"No one listens to The Dame either."

"Fantastic boss you have there then. Come on, Brad. Five minutes. All I need is five minutes with her."

"For what? Are you really thinking of leaving Kingsley for this middle-class Rotary club, as you called it?"

"I don't know. Maybe. Let me talk to The Dame. If she makes me an offer I can't refuse...well, then I won't refuse it."

"I do the recruiting for the club."

"Well then..." Nora took a step back and tapped her chin with the tip of her riding crop. She saw something heated and mischievous gleaming in Brad's dark eyes. "Maybe you should try to recruit me."

"I have Mistress Irina now, along with four other dominatrixes plus three male dominants, including me. We're not hiring any more doms."

"Pity. I have an impressive resume. And a huge client list. Everyone's on it."

"Everyone?"

"Your dad's on it."

Brad burst out laughing, and Nora only waited, her eyes wide with feigned innocence.

"You should be punished for bringing my father into this discussion," Brad said, raising a hand to her face. Nora didn't pull away. He might slap her. He might pinch her nose. He might even kiss her. She wouldn't have objected to any or all of those possibilities.

But instead of a slap or a pinch or a kiss, he simply caressed her cheek with his thumb. She started at the gentleness, the intimacy of the touch, and took a step back.

"What was that for?" she demanded, raising a hand to her face. The caress burned more than a slap would have.

"You're beautiful."

"And you're huge and handsome. You

don't see me going around getting all personal with your face."

"Would you like to get personal with my face?"

"I..." Nora stopped and swallowed. She needed to get back into control of this situation. She could handle Brad. She could handle any man. Well, except for one... "You're trying to top me, aren't you?"

"I told you. We're all stocked up on dommes. What we really need are a few good subs."

Nora's spine stiffened. "I don't sub."

"Not anymore, right?"

Nora glared at him.

"Come on, Nora. Everyone knows who you used to belong to. It's not a secret."

"Not a secret, no. But not anything I want to talk about."

"Was it all that bad, being a sub for him?"

Nora let her most dangerous smile spread across her face. "No. It was that good."

"Then you should enjoy doing it again."

"You're a big man, Brad, but not even you could fill his shoes."

"Worth a shot, isn't it? You want to meet The Dame, then you have to get through me."

"Through you? Or under you?"

"Both."

Nora fell silent and considered the offer. Wasn't like she'd never subbed before. She'd been a sub longer than she'd been a dominatrix—ten years she'd spent in a collar. Ten beautiful years. But she couldn't do that again. Could she?

"No collar," she said with finality. "One hour of you on top. I'll sub. Then I get my five minutes with The Dame."

Brad leaned against the stair railing and studied her with his pale blue eyes.

"Nora...we both know you're not going to leave King for Black Forest. Why are you so interested in talking to The Dame?"

"I have my reasons."

"Are you going to tell me your reasons?"

"Nope."

"Of course, if you submit to me, I suppose I could order you to tell me your reasons."

At the utterance of the words "submit to me," Nora's heart started to race a little faster, her breath quickened.

She licked her bottom lip in nervous anticipation. "Yes, I suppose you could."

"Call me 'sir' if you want to see The Dame," he ordered, pressing closer.

"So..." Nora stopped and took a breath, "what are our rules here...sir?"

"No rules."

"No rules? Not even..."

Brad grinned at her with such hunger Nora wasn't sure if he planned to beat her or eat her.

"I'll take that as a 'not even...'" Nora said. She took a long breath in and slowly let it out through her teeth. They didn't need to spell it out. No rules meant no rules. And the one rule of professional dominants? No sex with the clients. But she wasn't a client. She was a dominatrix, a dominatrix who really needed to get laid.

A month off.

No Kingsley.

No work.

Europe.

"Fine. Done. One hour. No rules. I'm yours."

Brad only stared at her with his lips a thin hard line. He raised his eyebrow. Once more Nora sighed.

"I'm yours...sir."

"You are now."

Brad didn't hesitate, no doubt not wanting to give her the chance to change her mind.

With his right hand he grasped Nora by her upper arm and half-dragged, half-carried her up the stairs. Nora dropped her eyes to the floor and let him lead her to a room near the end of the hallway. He kicked it open and threw her in. She landed on the plush carpeted floor and stayed there not looking at him while he closed and locked the door.

"When's the last time someone hit you?" Brad stood in front of her, his feet on either side of her knees.

"Been...awhile." She started to smile up at him but remembered her place.

"Too long. Look at you...dressed up like one of the big girls with her big girl boots. And trying to play with the big kids? It's embarrassing. Are you even thirty yet?"

"Thirty-one...sir."

"Are you even five-feet-tall?"

"Five-foot-three."

"You're a little girl, Nora. And someone needs to remind you that this town doesn't belong to you."

Brad reached down and tapped Nora under her chin, a signal that she was to look at him. She met his eyes and waited in silence.

"So this is how we get you to shut up." Brad grinned wickedly at her and desire coupled with rebellion welled up within her. "We should make you submit more often. Cross. Now."

Nora started to stand up, but Brad put a hand on her shoulder and pushed her back down.

"Crawl to it."

She hid her rolling eyes behind her hair and crawled on her hands and knees to the St. Andrew's cross on the wall.

"Up."

She stood up and waited as Brad unlaced her corset and pulled it off of her. It took a hard bite to her own tongue to stop herself from smirking as Brad stared at her now naked breasts.

"What a waste..." Brad sighed as he cupped her breasts in both large hands. The heat from his hands sunk into her skin. Nora almost sighed from the pleasure of his touch but didn't want to give him the satisfaction. "Such a beautiful woman...you should spend your days and nights naked tied to a man's bed, gagged and blindfolded with your body waiting to be used."

He kneaded her right nipple, and Nora closed her eyes.

"But instead Kingsley keeps you locked up

in leather." Brad kissed that sensitive spot under her ear as he unzipped her skirt. Nora suppressed a ragged breath. She didn't want to want this as much as she did. She had to control herself, stay focused, let him do what he wanted so she could get what she wanted and get out. But she couldn't quite remember what she wanted.

Brad pulled her skirt down and off her before touching her clitoris gently with the tip of his finger.

Oh yes. That was what she wanted. Now she remembered.

Naked but for her boots, Nora stood waiting as Brad assaulted her with the softest of kisses on her neck and shoulders, the most careful of touches on her breasts. His restraint was the purest form of torture for a woman who hadn't been fucked in two months.

"Turn around," he ordered but didn't wait for her to comply. He simply spun her and forced her into the X-shaped cross. Nora rested her cheek against the wall and waited. So many memories crowded into her mind...memories of nights she'd left behind with the one man, the only man she'd ever loved...

"Do you like it?" Brad asked as he strapped her wrists and ankles to the wood. "I made it myself."

"It's beautiful." Nora spoke with sincerity. She knew good work when she saw it. "Sturdy. I like the black paint. Looks a lot like the one in my basement at home."

"You keep a St. Andrew's cross in your basement? You're kinkier than I thought."

Nora shrugged. "It doubles as a drying rack."

"And that's a flogging for you." Brad pulled away, and Nora grinned into the crossbeam.

"Oh...darn."

She steeled herself as behind her Brad whipped the air with a flogger. From the sound of it, she could tell he'd picked a heavy one. It beat the air instead of slicing through it. This would hurt.

Good.

The first blow landed without a word of warning, but she managed to stifle any cries of pain or shock. The second landed even harder but still Nora keep quiet. Sadists and dominants loved forcing a reaction from their subs—pleasure, pain, shock, shame, it didn't matter as long as the submissive entertained them with their moans and gasps and pleas for mercy. But Nora wouldn't give Brad the satisfaction.

After a few minutes, he dropped the flogger, and Nora panted as quietly as she could while her back burned and ached. What would he do to her next? Caning maybe? A single-tail? A paddle? She'd had it all before. Nothing he did would shock her or surprise her.

From behind her she heard movement, the rustle of fabric. She gasped when Brad pressed his body against her back. She felt nothing but skin and desire against her.

"Now I know how to get a reaction out of you." Brad chuckled in her ear. His erection pressed into her. She felt a drop of something warm and wet on the small of her back.

"I promise...I'm reacting," she whispered as Brad ran his hands up and down the sides of her body...over her ribcage and waist, down her hips and thighs and up again. He slipped a hand between her open legs and shoved two fingers inside her. They went in easily, her wet body giving him no resistance.

"Good reaction."

"Thank you, sir."

Brad bit down into her neck hard enough she flinched. "And that was an even better one. Wonder what kind of reaction I'll get when I fuck you."

"Only one way to find out," Nora breathed as Brad pushed a third finger into her.

"Very true...you know, Nora, for that little stunt you pulled, keeping quiet while I was beating the hell out of you, I'm going to have to punish you. I think maybe I'll punish you by fucking you so hard you scream for me."

Now Nora laughed. "I don't scream, sir. I make others scream. In fact, that's how I ended up at the police station this morning."

"You don't scream? You say that like it's a fact," he said, unstrapping her from the cross, "when we both know I'll just take it as a challenge."

He dragged her from the cross to a small bed piled high with silk sheets and pillows. Pulling a pillow to the center of the bed, he pushed Nora onto it, positioning it under her hips as she laid face-down on the bed. She waited while he moved about the room gathering supplies. He was cute, Brad was. Scream? Her? During sex?

Brad came back to the bed and took both her wrists in one hand. First he looped black silk rope around them before tying them to one bedpost. She heard metal and felt Brad forcing her legs even wider apart. He clamped cuffs around her booted ankles and hooked them to the ends of a spreader bar. Nora breathed deep and let her hips open up and relax into the three-foot spread. Brad must be in the mood to go deep.

"Are you trying to make me scream from pleasure or pain?" Nora taunted. With her ankles so far apart, she'd probably feel Brad all the way against her bottom ribs. Fine. Let him fuck her like that. She could take and would take it...all the way to Europe for a month.

"Doesn't matter as long as you're screaming." She heard the dark amusement in his voice. Typical sadist—arrogant, superior, and casually brutal. They really were her favorite men.

Brad straddled her hips and Nora took a few slow, calming breaths. No one had been inside her for two months. And at this angle in this position...this wasn't going to be easy.

Close your eyes and think of England... Nora repeated Queen Victoria's famous wedding night advice to herself. England. France. Europe. Castles...dungeons...men who didn't speak English...the canals of Venice...water lapping at the sides of her boat...the wheels of trains passing through the Alps...the sounds of buzzing...

Buzzing?

Brad pushed a hand under Nora's hips and lifted them an inch off the pillow. She flinched with pleasure as he pressed a butterfly-style vibrator against her clitoris. A hand on her back guided her back down into the pillow, the vibrator firmly nestled against her, sending waves of bliss reverberating through her hips and stomach and thighs. Over the buzzing she heard the unmistakable sound of foil tearing.

Nora turned her face into the burgundy silk as Brad pressed his knees against hers. As wet as she was and as open, Nora took his full length into her easily. She groaned as he filled her inch by inch.

"That's a good start," he whispered in her ear. "I think we can turn the volume up a little though."

He punctuated the suggestion with a thrust, hard and deep. Nora gasped and pushed into the vibrator. Her clitoris pulsated with sensation. She pulled against the ropes that tied her to the bedpost.

"You can't get away..." Brad trailed kisses across her shoulders. He moved slowly inside her, pulling himself out to the tip before pushing back in. Nora's gasps turned to moans and back to gasps again. Brad set a steady pace and didn't deviate from it no matter how Nora moved underneath him. He kept her perched on the edge of ecstasy but didn't push hard enough to send her over. Instead he continued to thrust with precision and control. It seemed to go on forever. Nora felt herself rising off the bed as she fell into the rhythm of the sex. God, she missed this. And not only the penetration, the physical sensation, she missed being underneath a man, missed being dominated, being used. She shouldn't like this feeling so much. It put terrible thoughts in her head. Thoughts of him...the man who'd found her, made her, changed her, and loved her. The man she'd left and would never go back to.

Brad slipped his hands over her ribcage and cupped her breasts, holding them as he began to thrust harder into her. With such force she should have been moaning with pain, but the vibrator pulsed into her clitoris and the harder he pushed the more she wanted. Her breathing grew louder, more ragged, more desperate and hungry. She heard Brad's own grunts of pleasure in her ear. She let out a moan, deep and throaty, and Brad started to pound into her with brutal force. The pleasure slammed against pain and pushed back into pleasure. Brad reached under her and forced the vibrator even harder into her.

Nora buried her face in the sheets. Brad dug his teeth into the back of her shoulder. When she came, she came with a scream even the bed could not muffle. But not even her scream could cover the sound of Brad's groan as he flinched and shuddered with his own powerful orgasm.

Passively Nora lay beneath Brad as he caught his breath before pulling slowly out of her raw body. He untied her wrists from the bedpost, unstrapped her ankles from the spreader bar. Nora rolled onto her back, looked his naked form up and down, and laughed.

"Yes, laughing at me while I'm naked," Brad said as he looped the rope and knotted it neatly. Nora saw the amusement in his eyes. "That is sure to get you into my good graces."

"I'm only laughing because your nickname is so appropriate...Mr. Big Brad Wolfe," Nora said with nothing but appreciation for his big-Bradness. "Is Wolfe really your last name?"

Brad gave her a wink. "Is Nora Sutherlin really your name?"

"*Touché.* So it's been an hour. And you made me scream, you bastard. Do I win? Do I get my five minutes with the Dame?"

Brad sighed heavily. "Talking about your one motivation for letting me beat you and fuck you won't really get you on my good side either."

This time, Nora couldn't see the smile.

"Brad...you knew I was here to see the Dame. One hour with you, five minutes with her. That was the deal." Nora raised up on her elbows, wincing at the soreness between her legs.

"The deal. Right."

"You and me...we're supposed to be professionals here," she reminded him.

"I don't fuck my clients." Brad pulled on his pants with brisk efficiency. "Neither do you, I hear. What happened here wasn't business."

"Yeah...but it was a lot of fucking fun."

Brad finally cracked a smile. "I can't argue with that. Okay, get dressed. The Dame's office is opposite this one in the other hall—

black door, red knob. Don't bother knocking. Just go in."

"Will she be nice to me?"

"Depends on her mood. I'll see you out."

Brad left without even kissing her good-bye. Then Nora realized how odd it was she even wanted him to. Just sex. Just a trade. Just business. Right?

Careful of her flogged back, Nora dressed in her skirt and corset and pulled on her red cloak once more. She took her time for reasons she didn't want to consider. She needed to get this over with so she could get out of town and forget about Kingsley, about the Black Forest, and especially about the Big Brad Wolfe. She'd lay down her little red riding crop for a few weeks and come back to New York more vicious than ever.

Nora strode down the hall to the black door with red knob. After one quick breath, she turned the knob, stepped inside and felt her jaw hitting the floor.

When she finally picked it up again, she could only manage one single sentence.

"My goodness," Nora said to The Dame, "what a big...crop you have."

BRAD ESCORTED Nora to the door of the Black Forest.

"So what are you going to tell Kingsley?" he asked, running a hand up and down Nora's arm.

"I'll tell him the truth. I met The Dame. I talked to The Dame. The Dame promised to stop poaching King's people if King promises he'll stop sending spies into Black Forest."

"Very good. What if Kingsley asks what The Dame is like?"

Nora grinned up at Brad, up at the mysterious Dame who no one ever saw but everyone had heard of.

"Like I said, I'll tell him the truth. I'll tell him The Dame is amazing in bed."

"You can also tell Kingsley The Dame will send Hunt back to him if Kingsley's willing to give the poor boy two days off a week."

Nora nearly sagged with relief.

"You're giving Hunt back? I'm a better lay than I thought I was."

"Top five of my life. Definitely."

"Thank you, sir. You're not so bad yourself."

With a final grin thrown over her shoulder, Nora left the club and headed back to the real world, to the streets of Manhattan, the streets she couldn't wait to leave behind. All the way back to her house in Connecticut, Nora thought of Brad and the brilliant ruse of The Dame—the club owner no one ever saw but ruled her dark little world from behind the sheer curtains of Black Forest. She'd somehow earned Brad's trust, earned a glimpse behind that curtain. And more importantly, had earned her month off, her month in Europe.

She barely slept that night while trying to decide where she'd go, what she would do with all her time off. The next morning she packed fast, grabbed her passport and decided to book a ticket at the airport. Fate would decide her next move. She'd pick a destination based on the next flight out when she got there.

At Kingsley's townhouse, she picked up her last paycheck for four weeks and parked her car in his garage. In the cab, she told the driver to take her to JFK and drop her at any gate she wanted. Nora leaned back in the seat and closed her eyes. Freedom...she'd earned a month of freedom. No boss to tell her what to do, where to go, what people to beat. Exactly what she wanted, right? So why did she feel so uneasy?

The cab jolted as it hit a bump and Nora opened her eyes. "What happened?"

"Sorry, Miss. Construction. Had to take a detour," the driver said.

Nora nodded and looked out the window. To her right she saw none other than the entrance to Black Forest. She shifted uncomfortably in her seat as memories of Brad inside her body caused desire to well up inside her hips and stomach.

The cab started to inch forward and Nora let out a "Stop!" saying the word before she even knew why.

The driver slammed on the breaks. Nora grabbed her suitcase and threw a hundred through the window.

"I'm getting out here. Thanks."

Nora half-walked, half-ran to the door of Black Forest and knocked until her knuckles turned red.

The door flew open.

Brad stood staring at her. The stare turned into a smile that turned into a laugh that filled the Black Forest.

"My...what a big smile you have," Nora said, trying to rein in her own idiotic grin.

Brad grabbed her by the arm, pulled her

into the club, and slipped his hand under her skirt.

One kiss on the lips turned into another and another.

"Why..." he whispered as his mouth trailed down her body, "all the better to eat you with."

━━

THE LETTER

By their thirteenth date, Bryce decided to just make a game of it. Would it be tonight that Leigh dumped him? Tomorrow? Would they make it to fourteen dates? Fifteen? Why she kept saying "yes" to him when he asked her out was beyond him. On their second date, they'd kissed. On their fourth date, they'd made out on her sofa. After that, all progress toward consummation came to a screeching halt and entirely without explanation.

Dinner came. They ate it. Dessert came. They ignored it. Bryce studied Leigh over the top of his wine glass. Beautiful girl...red hair with streaks of brown and black, dark eyes that brightened with laughter...she had a freckle on her top lip that he loved to bite when she let him kiss her. On date twelve she hadn't let him kiss her. Tonight she wouldn't even look him in the eyes.

"Are you a virgin?" Bryce asked, deciding he had nothing to lose at this point. Clearly things were going nowhere. If he couldn't have her, maybe he could at least get some answers.

Leigh sat up straighter and gave him a look of profound shock. "No...of course not. Where—"

"Born-again virgin? Incredibly Catholic? Do you have an STD? HIV? Raging antibiotic resistant tuberculosis? If so, I'm willing to work around any and all of that."

Leigh laughed nervously and shook her head. "Bryce, I don't have—"

"Why haven't we slept together yet?"

She sat her wine glass on the table and crossed her arms over her chest.

"It's...complicated," she began and stopped. "I wish I could explain. I want to but when I try it's..." She brought a hand up to her lips and pulled at the air as if trying to drag reluctant words from her mouth.

Her body sagged and suddenly she looked so small and sad in the chair across from him that he wanted to drag her into his arms and apologize for even bringing it up. This girl...he fucking adored her. Her laugh, her smile, her dry sense of humor, the way her voice went all goofy and high-pitched when she played with his dog...he had to have her in his life. And she must have felt something, anything for him to keep saying "yes" to all these dates. So why...?

"Can't what? Can't tell me? Can't explain? Can't say it in any language other than French? That's fine. I'll learn French. Just tell me."

She shook her head. "I should never have said 'yes' to the first date, Bryce. And I'm sorry. People like us, like me...we usually don't go out with guys we meet at the gym."

She paused and growled as if profoundly frustrated with her own inability to explain. Bryce wondered what the hell she meant by "people like us."

"I like you so much that against my better judgment—" she continued.

"Oh, thank you very much for that."

"That's not what I mean." Leigh clenched her hands and groaned softly. That groan, he heard passion in it. Frustration. No way was this woman frigid. Exhaling through her nose, she looked up and met his eyes. "You're the nicest guy I've ever met. You're kind and sweet and chivalrous and gentle…"

"Horrible, I know."

"I'm not like you. I'm different. And I want to tell you how but I just can't get it out."

"Then write me a damn letter if you can't say it."

Leigh's eyes widened at the suggestion. "A letter? I can do that. I'll do that."

"You will?" He hadn't been serious. But the thought of a letter, the thought of any form of explanation for her strange behavior excited him. At this point knowing why she wouldn't sleep with him turned him on almost as much as her actually agreeing to sleep with him.

"Yes. I'll write it and mail it to you. It'll explain everything. And then you won't have to see me again once you know if you don't like what it says. You'll just know. And then we'll both feel better."

Bryce nodded in agreement. "Fine. Write the letter. But I promise you will see me again."

Leigh turned her head and stared down at the floor. She grabbed her sweater from the back of her chair, threw her purse over her shoulder, and stood up.

Looking at him, she gave him a wan smile.

"I really like you," she said. "So read the letter first. Don't promise me anything until you do."

And with those ominous words, she left the restaurant and maybe even his life.

For the next three days, Bryce rushed home from work and checked his mailbox before doing anything else. Nothing...nothing...nothing...Finally on day four, he held it in his hands. Pale pink envelope, black ink... the letter.

It took all of his willpower not to open it up and begin reading it right on the sidewalk. Shoving it in his pocket, he went inside, poured a glass of white wine, sat in his favorite chair and carefully sliced open the envelope.

The stationery matched the envelope— black ink on pale pink paper. Scanning the first page, Bryce saw no date at the top, no "Dear Bryce." His eyes fell onto the first sentence and he began to read...

———

NAKED SHE WAITED on the bed...knees to her chest, arms around her shins, head bowed and eyes closed. As instructed. As always. And as instructed she'd pulled her long hair into low pigtails that hung over her shoulders and tickled her collarbone. He seemed to love the combination of sweet and spice in her—her hair so girlishly dressed, her body naked, her eyes rimmed with black eyeliner in full Cleopatra mode. Anything he wanted she would do for him. She'd style her hair as he wanted, dress as he liked...anything for him. All it took was an order.

She stiffened slightly when she heard the bedroom door open. Closing her eyes tightly, she fought the need to look at him. God, she loved to look at him—at his black hair, slightly unruly, his bright blue eyes, the leather bracelet he wore along with his leather-banded watch. He'd always rolled his shirtsleeves to the elbows. Until him she'd never realized how erotic male forearms could be.

—————

BRYCE PAUSED IN HIS READING. He looked down at his shirt. As usual he'd rolled his shirtsleeves up to his elbow. On his left wrist a black leather bracelet accompanied his leather-band watch. He ran a hand through his black hair a few inches longer than his mother considered entirely respectable.

Wait...was Leigh writing about him? No way. They'd never...only in his dreams.

Bryce kept reading.

━━━

SHE INHALED SHARPLY when his hands came to her shoulders and rested there for a moment. From her shoulders they slid higher until he held her by her neck, his fingers lightly pressed into the hollow of her throat. Her entire body came alive at his touch both gentle and threatening. His hands fell away from her and then it was his lips on her neck instead. And then a collar, her leather collar that he always buckled around her neck before taking her—a sign of possession. He owned her. This was proof.

He trailed kisses from her ear to shoulder and back up again. She flinched as his teeth met her earlobe.

"Hands and knees," he ordered in a whisper. Without hesitation she rolled forward and into position.

His hands traced a path down her back, over her hips, down and up her thighs. His fingers found her labia and he opened the delicate folds wide...wider...She knew he was looking at her and studying the most private parts of her. Her skin flushed, but not with embarrassment. Only with desire.

Two fingers he pushed into her. He went deep until he found the core of her. A small sigh escaped her lips as he pulled his fingers out.

Then all the gentleness disappeared.

With one hand he forced her onto her chest as he yanked her arms behind her back. Cold metal ringed her wrists—handcuffs. He pulled her roughly up to her knees and dragged her to the floor.

"Knees," he ordered and she went down without hesitation. He opened his pants, took her by the chin, and forced himself into her mouth.

She loved the size of him, the feel of him in her mouth, the slight salt taste of him against her tongue. Slowly he thrust in and out while she sucked and caressed and kissed. Ostensibly she was his property. At moments like this, however, she knew she owned him, too.

His breathing quickened and she readied herself to swallow. Instead he pulled out of her mouth, grabbed her by the shoulder, and dragged her once more to her feet.

"You enjoyed that, didn't you?" he rasped the words in her ear.

"Yes, sir."

"Because you like sucking cock? Or because you like sucking my *cock?"*

She smiled. "Yes, sir."

He laughed softly and nipped at her neck. "Good answer."

She stood still and waited as he undressed. She wanted to watch, wanted to see him but kept her eyes respectfully lowered to the floor. Only her respect for him, for his dominance, his mastery of her eclipsed her desire for him. Everything primal and female in her wanted to lay itself at the feet of everything male and primitive in him.

———

BRYCE COUGHED AND ADJUSTED HIMSELF. Leigh had written this? It was like something straight out of a Nora Sutherlin novel. He took a large drink of his wine and considered turning the A/C up in the house. Suddenly it had gotten incredibly warm in his living room.

———

WITH A HAND on the back of her neck, he steered her to the closed closet door. As a birthday gift to her, he'd gotten an over-the-door restraint system. Now he had somewhere to tie her up. Made for much easier flogging.

He took off the handcuffs and tossed them aside before forcing her arms over her head. One by one he buckled each of her wrists to the straps on the door. She turned her head and rested her cheek against the cool painted wood. In and out she breathed, slowly...deeply...She let herself fall into a meditative trance that even the first fall of the flogger on her back didn't interrupt. But the second, much harder lash did. She grunted with every new strike. Her back burned with pain. Her body burned with need. She wanted it to go on forever. She needed it to stop immediately.

He dropped the flogger and pushed his chest into her back. At first she flinched from the pain but the feel of his warm body on her ravaged back sent renewed desire singing through her skin.

When he unstrapped her from the door and pushed her onto the bed, she felt only relief. Finally...at last...

"Stomach," he ordered and she rolled over and spread her legs. She loved to spread for him, to offer her body to him and let him take her any way he wanted. Straddling her hips, he pushed inside her and started to thrust. Underneath him she lay almost motionless as he used her body for his own pleasure. He clamped his hands over her wrists and pinned her hard against the bed as he moved harder and faster inside her. She tried to ignore how her body responded to his every movement, his every touch...the tip of his cock grazed her g-spot and she gasped into the sheets...his mouth caressed the sensitive center of her back... She wanted to raise her hips and take him even deeper inside her, let him make her come. But this time was for him and him alone. And she loved to give herself over to him to be used solely to satisfy his own needs. His breathing grew louder. His grip on her wrists tightened to the point of pain.

"Bite," he ordered and she brought her mouth to his forearm and dug her teeth into his skin. With a long shudder he came inside her as her mouth continued to mark the occasion on his arm.

He exhaled and she relaxed back into the sheets. She hadn't broken the skin but he would have a beautiful bright red bite mark on his arm for the next week. Knowing him, he'd take a picture of it and email it to her tomorrow with a little note that confessed he grew hard every time he looked at the bruise.

With casual strength, he flipped her onto her back. He kissed her breasts, sucked lightly and then harder on her nipples. Gripping her knees, he forced her legs wide-open and pushed two fingers into her again. His fingers moved easily inside her *as wet as she was with her arousal and his semen. A third finger joined the other two. The shock of pleasure sent her hips rising off the bed. He turned his hand inside her and pinned her back down against the mattress as he brought his lips to her clitoris. With his hand he rubbed her g-spot, massaged her labia, moved in and out of her with spiraling circles that sent he reeling while his lips and tongue tasted her, explored her, brought her to the edge and left her hovering there...finally he let her fall off the edge but caught her before she landed.*

He kissed his way up her stomach, over her ribcage, across her chest, and up to her lips. Their mouths met finally and she tasted herself on his tongue.

Pulling up he gazed down at her and brushed a tendril of hair off her forehead.

"My little girl," he whispered. "Mine."

"Yours, sir..." she sighed and closed her eyes.

———

BRYCE REACHED the end of the letter and immediately started over reading it from the beginning.

So this was her? This woman who wanted to be owned, used, flogged, tied up, taken, possessed...this was Leigh? This was the woman who hadn't even slept with him after two months and thirteen dates? This wildly sexual, confident, erotic woman?

*I'm different...*those were her words at dinner. Bryce shook his head. The woman had told him "no" not because she was a virgin or religious or scared...but because she was kinky and needed to be with someone like her.

You're the nicest guy I've ever met. You're kind and sweet and chivalrous and gentle...

Leigh was kinky and she thought he wasn't. And that's why she hadn't gone to bed with him in all this time. For weeks she'd wanted to tell him what she was but she'd been too embarrassed, too shy. And even now she hadn't told him. She'd shown him instead. And from the almost painful erection pressing against the fly of his pants, it was clear he'd liked what he saw.

In seconds, Bryce was out of the door and in his car. Racing across town, he made it to her apartment in record time.

He pounded on the door and Leigh answered it with wide, wary eyes.

"Bryce...what is—"

Before she could finish the sentence, he clamped a hand over her mouth, stepped inside the apartment, and kicked the door shut behind him.

Shoving her against the wall, Bryce locked his legs against hers, immobilizing her.

"Don't scream," he ordered as he lowered his hand from his mouth. Already she'd begun to breathe heavily. Sliding a hand between their bodies, he reached under her skirt, pushed the fabric of her panties aside, and slid a single finger into her. She burned against his hand, already wet for him. "Still think I'm too nice for you?"

She swallowed. "No."

"That was you in the letter." He moved his finger in and out of her as she began to pant. "But you didn't name him. Was that me? Or your dream man?"

A slight smile played at the corner of her lips. "Yes, sir."

Bryce brought his mouth to her neck and bit her hard enough to make her whimper. He hoped she had nowhere to go tonight. He didn't plan to let her go until dawn.

"Good answer."

THE ASSISTANT

"What would you say to a three-day weekend?" Lennon asked, and Ivy could have rung his beautiful neck for even suggesting such a thing.

"Why?" she asked, turning from the filing cabinet in his private office to face him. She'd been digging for something she hadn't actually needed, which she did about five times a day simply to have an excuse to go into Lennon's office.

"Why? You don't say 'Why?' when your boss offers you a three-day weekend. You say, 'Hell yes, boss. Best idea I've ever heard.'"

Ivy pursed her lips at him. "Why?" she asked again.

"You and I both worked all weekend last weekend," Lennon said, leaning back in his vintage leather swivel chair. He put his hands behind his head and raised his eyebrows, waiting for her to contradict him. Ivy envied the hands on his hair. Lennon was a young silver fox, and didn't seem to mind at all that he was mid-thirties and already mostly gray.

"No big deal." She waved her hand and sat in the club chair across from his desk. When she crossed her legs, she watched him, hoping he'd look at her legs. He did for a split second before meeting her eyes again. "It's not like you didn't pay me overtime." And it's not like she hadn't loved every second of it. Weekend work meant Lennon out of a suit and in jeans and his favorite ratty concert T-shirts. Saturday had been Pink Floyd. Sunday belonged to Eminem.

Lennon leaned forward, rested his elbows on his desk and looked her in the eyes. Blue eyes, bright but tired.

"Katie broke up with me," he said.

"What? Why?" Breaking up with Lennon seemed as insane as setting a Rembrandt on fire. Who did that?

"This is awkward." Lennon wrinkled his face up, and it was as handsome wincing as it was smiling.

"Me?" Ivy asked.

"She said I spent more time with my assistant than I do with her."

"You do."

"If you weren't, you know, you, it wouldn't be a problem. But you are you and that's a problem. For her, not me."

"Did you just tell me I'm pretty?"

Lennon glared at her. "You know you are. Katie wouldn't care about that if I didn't spend my weeks with you *and* my weekends with you. She says you're my work wife."

Then make me your real wife, you beautiful idiot.

"So why the three-day weekend? You trying to get rid of me?" Ivy asked.

"Never," he said vehemently, and she cherished that vehemence. "Jack's taking me out tomorrow for a recovery day of hiking and drinking. Then he's forcing me entirely against my will to go to a party at a friend's house Saturday night. And if I'm not here, there's no reason for you to be here."

"Three-day weekend it is then." Ivy stood up and smoothed her skirt down. "And thank you. I got invited to a party too this weekend," she said, a lie. It wasn't a party so much as brunch with her sister. "Maybe it's the same party as yours."

Lennon stood up and walked around his desk. Gently he lifted the little gold Star of David pendant she wore on a necklace. His fingers were so light on her skin she felt goosebumps all over her arms. And Lennon stood so close she could smell his light cologne.

"No offense, but I don't think you go to the same parties Jack and I go to. Although if you want to come with us, you can. Beautiful women are always welcome at that house." He said it like a dare, like a challenge.

"Is it one of *those* parties?" Ivy asked as Lennon played with the six corners of the star. They were as comfortable with each other as people who worked in close quarters had to be. She'd smack his hand when he reached for her food. He'd let her sleep on his shoulder when they took red-eye flights to London. But this little moment felt different, felt personal.

"One of those parties, yeah…" He looked a little embarrassed and she adored him for it. He'd been careful to keep his personal life separate from his professional life, even with her. But one Sunday afternoon she'd had to run to his apartment for reasons entirely work-related, and while he'd been on the phone in the other room, she'd glanced through a half-open door and seen Lennon's bedroom. A leather flogger sat on the pillow and handcuffs dangled from the headboard. When Lennon had caught her looking he'd blushed and stammered an apology. She'd told him she didn't care as long as what he was doing in his free time was consensual. It had been the first thing she'd thought of to say and only later had she realized it made her sound boring, virginal and utterly vanilla. What she'd wanted to say was, *The handcuffs? The flogger? Lennon, that's nothing to apologize for. It's sexy as hell, and I volunteer as your next victim.* There hadn't been a night since she hadn't fallen asleep dreaming of his body, that bed, and those handcuffs on her wrists while she made herself come.

Ivy wrapped her hand around his fingers holding her pendant. "Lenn—"

Lennon let the pendant go like it had burned him. "You work for me," he said.

"I know. I know." She raised her hands in surrender.

She knew. She knew. They'd had this discussion once before on a night flight when neither of them could sleep but seemingly the rest of the plane could. He'd admitted his attraction to her, and she to him, and the only thing that had stopped them from joining the Mile-High Club had been Lennon's innate sense of decency that kept him from sleeping with an employee ten years his junior. She knew if she made the first move it would happen. But she just couldn't bring herself to do it.

Lennon took a step back. She stopped herself from taking a step forward. "Have a good three-day weekend. I'll see you on Monday."

Ivy smiled. "Monday."

Then she took her file, walked out of his office, and sat at her desk. She didn't trust herself to walk back into Lennon's office without declaring her love and/or lust for him, so instead she opened their messenger app and typed, *Need car service for the party? Where? When?*

Lennon wrote back thirty seconds later. *Yes, please. Saturday at 9. 152 Riverside Drive. Warn the driver we'll be dressed weird.*

How weird? she typed back.

Eyes Wide Shut weird.

I'll make a note the comment field.

And that's when it hit Ivy—she knew where the party was. She knew when it was. She knew she could go to it if she wanted to go to it.

She wanted to go to it.

Lennon had said *"Eyes Wide Shut* weird" and implied he'd be dressed in some sort of costume. That would make it much easier to slip in and out. She didn't want to do anything but see him, and be part of his world for a little while. She wouldn't even talk to him. But to pass unobserved she'd have to dress the part herself. Saturday morning she made an appointment with her stylist who did her hair in a complicated and very un-Ivy updo. She bought a slinky white dress and a white masquerade mask. Lennon had never seen her wear her hair like this. He'd never seen her wear white. And with the mask covering half her face, he'd have no idea it was her. Since it was one of "those" parties, Ivy also invested in a pair of white seamed stockings and a garter belt and white high heels with white ribbons that tied at the ankle. Once dressed she looked the opposite of her usual work self. Her own mother wouldn't recognize her.

When nine o'clock rolled around, she grabbed a cab. On her way there she told herself that if the party wasn't her scene, all she had to do was turn around and leave. She could do this. Get in, get out, don't cause trouble. Don't reveal herself and whatever she did, no contact with Lennon. None.

The cab dropped her off, and she paid her driver. It took her a couple seconds to work up the courage to step out and climb the stairs of the black-and-white three-story townhouse. Through the door she could hear the sounds of music and laughter and the usual party revelry going on inside. Before she knocked she tried the knob and found the door unlocked. As quickly and quietly as she could, Ivy stepped inside.

Oh.

Oh…

Oh, no.

Lennon hadn't been exaggerating. It really was one of *those* kinds of parties.

Everywhere she looked she saw couples coupling. Kissing in doorways, draped over each other on sofas and in the room to the left, some sort of sitting room, she saw a woman kneeling on her hands and knees on a coffee table while a man in a dark three-piece suit and devil horns fucked her from behind. They weren't alone in the room, not at all. People stood around watching, cheering. Someone even held a stopwatch in his hand. Cash was scattered on the table around the woman's hands and knees. From what Ivy could tell it was a contest and the devil was contestant number two. The previous contestant had fucked the woman twelve minutes and sixteen seconds before coming. The current contestant just fucked his way past the ten minute mark. Someone in the crowd said they were neck-in-neck. Someone else said they were cock-in-cock.

Ivy stared, mesmerized by the scene. It was porn—beautiful, erotic, playful live porn—and she couldn't look away. Her nipples tightened under her low-cut dress and her pussy swelled at the sight of the woman taking the cock so casually in a room of a dozen people. Ivy flushed and felt herself growing wet, and her vagina clenched at nothing, wanting something inside it.

"Want to play?" came a French-accented voice from behind her.

She turned and saw the man who'd spoken. He wore a military-style long coat, white shirt open at the collar, plus breeches and Hessian boots polished to a high shine. He was impossibly handsome, with shoulder-length, dark, wavy hair and a wolfish gleam in his dark eyes.

"I...no. Just watching," she said.

"I shouldn't play anyway," he said with a dramatic sigh. "I always win. Hardly fair, is it?" He lifted her hand to his lips at if to kiss the back of it. Instead he flipped her hand over and pressed his lips to the center of her palm. With a wink he walked away, no doubt seeking out more amenable prey.

Ivy turned to leave and came face to bare chest with a man wearing nothing but leather pants. Nothing. Not even shoes. He had shaggy hair, brown skin and a wicked smile. She felt a sudden pang of attraction to him.

"Oh, sorry," she said. "I—"

"You must be new," he said, narrowing his eyes at her.

"I'm very new. Very, very new."

"We like newbies around here." He cupped her chin. "Tell me what you want, and I'll make sure you get it."

Ivy opened her mouth, closed it, then saw Lennon striding down the hallway toward the front door. He wasn't dressed nearly as oddly as everyone else at the party. He had on black trousers, a black vest, and a white shirt with the cuffs rolled to his elbows. His only nod to the party atmosphere was the black mask he wore over his eyes. Impossible not to know it was him, however. Not with that smile and that salt-and-pepper hair.

"Him," Ivy whispered. "I want him."

"You sure about that?" the man in the leather pants asked. She couldn't believe she'd spoken her wish aloud.

"I am."

"Then kiss me."

Ivy kissed the stranger and found his mouth warm and his lips skillful. She'd been so busy with work for Lennon she hadn't gone on a date in six months. Whoever this man was, she didn't know, but she also didn't care. He had big hands that felt good on her waist, and a girl needed kissing sometimes. Even by a stranger.

And then Ivy was off her feet. Entirely, completely and totally off her feet, being carried over the man's shoulder.

"Oh my God," she said, and the man heard her.

"I'm a firefighter in real life," he said, slapping her on the ass. "Trust me, I know what I'm doing."

"Glad one of us does."

"Come on, man," he said as he carried her into a room. "I caught something for you."

"Aw, you shouldn't have, Jack." Ivy recognized Lennon's voice.

"You've had a hard week. You've earned some fun."

So this was Jack, Lennon's kinky friend who dragged him to parties? Is this something they did together? Share women? Ivy wanted to be jealous if it was, but instead she found the prospect arousing, the thought of being passed back and forth between them.

Ivy gripped the sofa cushion hard and tried to get her bearings. She was in a room, a very nice but small room with antique furniture like out of *Pride & Prejudice* or something. Door closed. No lights on but for the fire burning in the fireplace. No bed. Fireplace with an ornate, dark-wood mantel and a low fire burning. Other than the couch she and Jack sat on, there was one armchair across from them and a huge steamer trunk that acted as a coffee table. Lennon sat in the chair and held his wine glass lightly between his fingertips. He was watching her.

"This is how it works," Jack was saying as he slowly eased her panties down her legs. "Since you're new...I do whatever I want to do to you and you say 'Red' when and if you want me to stop. And what I want to do to you is fuck you while my friend watches. Then he will do whatever he wants to do you. He won't be nearly as gentle with you as I will. Yes? No? Red?"

Ivy glanced at Lennon, who grinned at Jack's warning.

She was scared, her heart pounding, her blood pumping so hard in her ears it sounded like the roar of an ocean.

"Yes."

She whispered the word so Lennon couldn't recognize her voice. But Jack heard.

"Good answer," he said, and casually unzipped his pants to pull out his cock.

He reached for a condom from the bowl of them on the steamer trunk. She couldn't believe this was happening as he stroked himself to his full hardness and rolled on the condom so matter-of-factly he could have been tying his shoes if he'd been wearing any.

"You can say 'red' anytime," Lennon said from his armchair. "We're big boys. We have self-control."

Ivy nodded her understanding, taking comfort in his words. It made it easier when Jack pushed her legs wide open. Out of the corner of her eye she could see Lennon leaning forward, lifting his chin to see her better. Since she'd gotten a full wax yesterday, she knew he could see everything—her open labia, her clitoris, her wetness—and it aroused her even more to know Lennon was seeing her body without even knowing it was hers. Jack inserted his index finger into her and rubbed along the walls of her vagina.

"New and eager," Jack said with a dirty grin, clearly impressed by how wet she was. She realized quickly he wasn't talking to her, but Lennon. "I'll open her up for you. You finish her off. Sound like a plan?"

Lennon answered, "A perfect plan."

Jack gripped her by the back of the knees and knelt between her thighs. This was happening...it was actually happening...Ivy breathed quick, shallow breaths to calm herself. It didn't work. Jack had his cock in his hand, and the tip pushed against her clitoris. A spasm of pleasure shot through her, and Ivy instinctively lifted her hips to offer herself to him. With one smooth stroke he was inside her. He pushed her dress up to her stomach, gripped her waist and rode her with firm steady thrusts. She couldn't believe she was doing this, letting a strange man fuck her while her boss watched. She lifted her head and watched Jack's cock pumping in and out of her. No denying it—she was doing this. Her head fell back on the sofa and she turned toward Lennon. She didn't mean to meet his eyes but as soon as she did, she couldn't look away. *See me,* she wanted to say to him. *Look at me. I'm not who you think I am. I'm not just your assistant. I'm a woman, and I need you like this...*

He saw her. Those blue eyes of his never left hers as Jack fucked her. If only he knew it was her. *It's me,* she told him with her eyes. *It's Ivy, and I want you enough I did this for you, to be with you...*

Jack was fucking her hard now, and Ivy opened her legs wider for him. Lennon moved from the chair and sat on the steamer trunk next to them. She wasn't ready for him to touch her, but touch her he did, pressing his hand onto her lower stomach and pushing down as if trying to feel Jack's cock moving inside her. Then Lennon dipped his fingertips into his white wine and touched her clitoris with them. She inhaled sharply, nearly flinching at the sudden coolness on her burning body. He grinned as he rubbed the swollen knot of flesh, toying with it at first before giving it the serious attention it needed. Her hips moved in tight circles as Lennon touched her and Jack fucked her. All sensation was concentrated in her pelvis, in her sex. Lennon worked her clitoris with two fingers and it more than she could take. This man she adored and lusted after touching her so intimately while she was being fucked... she came with a cry and a shudder, her hole gripping and grabbing at Jack's cock still pounding her. He slammed his orgasm into her as Ivy lay back, closed her eyes and took it.

She was empty inside again and her body felt warm and drowsy. Somewhere she heard a door open and close. Ivy was being lifted into strong arms. Limp and spent, she let the strong arms pull her upright and press her into the back of the couch. Thighs nudged her legs open and someone penetrated her again. Ivy opened her eyes and found herself in Lennon's arms, her chin on his shoulder, her legs wound around his waist, as he pinned her to the back of the couch with his cock inside her.

His hands were on her back, lowering the zipper on her dress. She stiffened, suddenly wide awake.

"We're alone," Lennon said, kissing her bare shoulder as he slid the straps of her dress down her arms. Down, down it went until he'd pushed her dress to her waist, baring her breasts for him. "Don't be shy."

Shy? She was finally having sex with the man she'd adored for two years. Ivy leaned back, arching for him, offering her breasts to him. He ran his hands over them, squeezing them lightly, holding them in his palms as he licked and sucked her nipples. Lennon was sucking her nipples and it felt better than anything had ever felt in her life. Fucking her softly at first, deeply, and then harder and harder. Jack had warned her Lennon would be rougher with her than he was. But Jack hadn't warned her it would feel this good. He was fucking her so hard now she could feel it in her stomach. She loved it, needed it, had needed it ever since she went to work for Lennon. He pulled out of her but only to turn her, bending her over the sofa arm. He entered her from behind and fucked her deep, his hands holding her breasts and squeezing them, tugging the nipples until she moaned.

"You like this?" he asked, and his voice sounded so unlike him. So forceful and dominant.

"Yes."

"When I'm done fucking you I'm going to flog you. Then fuck you again. You want that?"

She was so wet from his thrusts she felt it dripping down her thighs. "Yes."

"I knew you would."

But how did he know? He didn't even know it was her.

He didn't know...

"Red," Ivy said.

Lennon pulled out of her immediately as Ivy yanked her dress back up.

"What's wrong?" he asked, looking scared, concerned. He touched her arm. "I didn't hurt you, did I?"

"No," she said, scrambling off the sofa. "I'm sorry."

He reached for her again as she headed for the door, but she kept walking away from him and out of the house.

What was she thinking, having sex with her own boss without telling him it was her? Jack knew he was having anonymous sex with a girl he'd never met before. But Lennon didn't, and that wasn't right. No matter how much she wanted him, how good it felt, it wasn't right.

———

BY MONDAY MORNING, Ivy had pulled herself together as best as she could. She dressed in her normal clothes, did her hair the normal way, prepared to act as normally as she could. She wouldn't blow her cover. She wouldn't confess. She wouldn't put Lennon in a horribly awkward position because she'd followed him to his party like some lovesick puppy. She would be a grown-up and carry the secret. In the break room she poured two cups of coffee and marched into his office like it was any other day.

"Morning," she said, handing him his coffee.

"How was your weekend?"

"Good. Yours?" Ivy asked, keeping her face empty of expression.

"Good. Too short."

"Typical, right?"

"Right. But back to work. Can you bring me the Close Brothers file?"

She walked to the filing cabinet and

opened the top drawer. When she pulled out the file, something fell out onto the floor.

Ivy bent to pick it up and found a black mask in her hand. She looked at it, then looked at Lennon who was smiling smugly at her with his hands clasped behind his head.

"You tan easily, you know," he said. "But your Star of David pendant blocks the sun. You have a six-pointed pale spot on your chest."

"You knew it was me?"

"The whole time…"

"I didn't mean to. Jack was there and he asked me what I wanted and I said you. What's going to happen?" Ivy's heart pounded outside her chest, the mask clutched in her hand, memories of his mouth on her breasts and his fingers on her clitoris setting her to blushing and flushing and burning inside and out.

Lennon stood up and walked over to her. As he passed the door, he closed it and locked it.

"What would you say to a four-day week-end?" he asked.

Before she could answer, he dipped his head and kissed her slow and deep and long, his tongue touching hers, his hands on her lower back and roaming lower, and his hips pushing into hers. She pulled back from the kiss and stared up at him. He knew. And she knew. And they'd done it anyway. And now they were going to do it again.

"I would say…hell yes, boss. Best idea I've ever heard."

TYING THE KNOT

That they called him at all was the first bad sign. Bryce stepped into the house that he'd been banished from three days ago and looked around. Tulle everywhere. Sequins everywhere. Roses everywhere. And from upstairs came the sound of tears.

"Oh thank God," said Janice as she came down the staircase, a handkerchief pressed to her chest. "She won't listen to anybody."

"How bad is it?" Bryce stepped over a box of wine glasses that someone had left in the foyer.

"Bad." Janice shook her head. "She hasn't stopped crying for an hour. The shoes…it was the shoes that sent her over the edge."

Bryce raised his hand to silence Janice. The crying grew louder, turned briefly into panting as the weeper tried to regain control of herself, before dissolving once more into tears.

The second bad sign.

"Get everyone out of the house," he ordered Janice. "I need to be alone with Leigh."

Nodding, Janice picked the box of wine glasses off the floor. "I'll come back in an hour to pick her up. Is that enough time?"

Bryce thought about the possibilities, what he could do, what he should do...

"More than enough. But Janice?"

"Yes?"

"Knock first."

Janice took Leigh's ten-year-old niece by the hand. Two other women, Leigh's best friend and her favorite coworker, both barely glanced at him as they pulled on coats around puffy blue dresses.

"Good luck," Janice said.

"Don't worry," Bryce said, already halfway up the stairs. "I got this."

Bryce found his fiancée in a pile of white satin underwear on the floor, her mascara running in miserable rivulets down her otherwise beautifully painted face.

"No. No, no, no..." Leigh covered her face with her hands. "You aren't supposed to see me. Not now. Not like this. Not ever."

Sighing, Bryce squatted in front of her and cupped her chin with his hand, forcing her to meet his eyes.

"I've seen you in white before. I've seen you in tears before. Seeing you right now isn't going to doom the wedding."

"But—"

"But the bride having a nervous breakdown two hours before the ceremony might."

She gave a little pathetic laugh and hiccupped on her tears. Had she ever looked smaller, more vulnerable, more desirable before? If so, he couldn't remember when.

"Shoes? This is over shoes, young lady?" He let his voice turn stern. She always responded best to his most fatherly tone.

"They're green…" She grabbed a high heel and brandished it in his face.

"So?"

"The dresses are blue. The dye job's…it's totally wrong."

"So? Go barefoot. You. The bridesmaids. Everyone. Hell, I'll go barefoot. People will think it's sweet, eccentric. We'll pretend it's on purpose."

"But—"

"Will our marriage be null and void if the shoes don't match?"

Leigh only stared at him a moment before shaking her sad head. Long chestnut curls fell across her shoulders.

"No."

"Then fuck the shoes."

"But—"

"One more 'but' and I'm going to fuck the bride too."

Leigh's breath caught in her throat. She always gasped when he used such language with her.

"But you aren't even supposed to see me before the wedding, much less—"

"And that was another 'but.' Up."

Bryce stood up and waited. She didn't move.

"I'm not kidding, Leigh. Get off the floor right this second."

For a woman in seven layers of white pet-ticoats and four-inch high heels, Leigh got to her feet with impressive speed. Careful of the fabric, Bryce peeled it off her body until she stood naked in front of him.

Taking her by the wrist, he pulled her to the bed and she lay on her back. Leigh crossed her arms over her chest and stared up at the ceiling. He loved when she played martyr like this, played the innocent scared virgin to his wicked ravishing rake.

Bryce grasped her ankle and yanked her to the side of the mattress. From underneath the bed he pulled out a suitcase and quickly unzipped it.

"Glad your mother didn't go digging under our bed while she was here."

"I told her that's where I kept the naked pics of you."

Bryce smiled his approval at her lie. There were no naked pictures of him in the house. And the naked photos of her weren't under the bed—they were on his iPhone.

"Did you have to explain that?" he asked, pointing to the hook screwed into the ceiling above the bed. They'd seen a similar set-up at the dungeon they'd visited in New York City. Everything he knew about throwing a flogger, he'd learned from Mistress Irina.

Leigh smirked. "I said the previous owners had a lot of hanging houseplants."

"Wicked girl..." Bryce chastised, pulling a two-foot spreader bar and a length of rope from the suitcase. "Lying to your mother. You might have to be punished for that."

Leigh watched him with wary eyes as he

unbuckled his belt and pulled it free of his pants.

"But—" she began, and that's all Bryce let her get out.

"Butt exactly. Time for something blue." With a snap of his fingers, he ordered her onto her stomach. With his belt he landed one...two...three...quick hard strikes on her bottom and a fourth across the back of her thighs. "Now if that doesn't make you stop stressing about shoes, I don't know what will."

"What are shoes?" Leigh asked as Bryce threw his belt to the floor and rolled her onto her back.

"They go on your feet," he said.

"What are feet?" Leigh giggled as Bryce wrapped leather cuffs around her ankles.

"They're the parts of your body that belong on my shoulders. Remember?"

She met his eyes and smiled shyly at him. "Oh yeah...now I remember," she whispered.

Quickly, Bryce threaded the rope through Leigh's ankle cuffs and tied a knot to hold the rope taut. He cuffed her feet to each end of the spreader bar before hoisting her legs into the air. He loved her like this—tied up, immobile, her body belonging to him and him alone.

Dropping to his knees he gently licked her open folds. He tasted the sweetness of her desire for him and the sweat of her nervousness. His poor little girl...he knew they should have eloped. But Leigh had a bad habit of trying to please everyone. Someday she'd understand she had no one to please but herself and him. And she pleased him every single day...

He pushed his tongue into her vagina to get her as wet as possible. He moved his mouth to her clitoris and sucked gently on it as he inserted his fingers into her and kneaded her g-spot. Leigh bucked and moaned as he pushed in a third finger, then a fourth. She loved being penetrated, would even beg for it when he withheld it to punish her. But he couldn't withhold himself from her today. In two hours they'd be married—joined spiritually and legally into one. But what mattered now was to be joined physically, sexually...and the sooner, the better.

Leigh's breathing quickened as Bryce pushed his fingers even deeper into her wet heat. Her muscles tightened around his hand. He kneaded her clitoris even harder with his tongue until her whole body went taut and she cried out, her fluid pouring from deep within her and over his face.

By the time he got back to his feet, he'd already opened his pants and freed his erection. He didn't even let Leigh catch her breath. He shoved himself into her hard and deep, thrusting without mercy or apology. He wanted her raw from sex when she walked down the aisle, every step reminding her of his desire for her.

He kissed her calves, her ankles as he pumped his hips furiously against her. With the arrival of friends and family, he'd been banished to a hotel three days ago. Now he had three-days of pent-up need within him. He thrust three times as hard, three times as long, and finally, when he came with his eyes shut tight, he poured three times the semen into her.

After catching his breath, he pulled out of Leigh and cleaned himself off as she lay panting on the bed, her legs still up in the air tied to the spreader bar. Bryce found Leigh's abandoned white panties and brought them back to the bed.

He unhooked her ankles from the bar and rested them on his shoulders. Slowly, he slid the satin panties down her legs and over her hips.

"Don't you dare take a shower between now and the wedding," he ordered as she removed her ankle cuffs and put all their supplies away under the bed.

Leigh rolled up and wrapped her arms around his shoulders. He held her close and tight and hated that he had to let her go now.

"Yes, sir," she whispered.

He dipped his head and dropped slow kisses onto each nipple before kissing her lips.

"Now get dressed, forget the shoes, and if you get stressed again, just think about my cock in your mouth, your pussy, and your ass...in that order."

"In other words, think about the wedding night?"

"Exactly."

━━

Later that day...

BRYCE STOOD BAREFOOT and waiting at the altar as the music began and, one by one, equally barefoot bridesmaids walked down the aisle. He didn't even glance at them, didn't even see the two hundred assembled guests, didn't even see the groomsmen at his side. He saw only Leigh as she appeared in the doorway bathed in sunlight and smiles. From under her dress he saw her naked toes peeking out. And he knew his semen still lingered inside her, private proof that she belonged to him already.

"That's my girl," he said softly to her as she reached the altar.

"Now and always."

The reverend stepped forward and cleared his throat. "You two ready to tie the knot?" he asked in a whisper.

"Definitely," Leigh said.

Bryce nodded at him and took a breath.

"For the second time today."

―――

The Butterfly. Cowgirl. Missionary. Doggy.

Lela flipped page after page after page in the sex-position manual and grew more and more depressed with every picture that greeted her. All of them. She'd done every single last position in the book.

Tears of frustration burned her eyes. She blinked rapidly to dispel them, but one escaped and landed in the center of a Lotus position sex diagram.

"Dammit." She hastily wiped off the tear but it had already left a watermark. Now she had to buy the stupid thing.

"I've seen women crying into books before, but usually it's over in the fiction section," came a voice from behind her.

Turning around, Lela came face to chest

with a man over six feet tall. Craning her neck, she found his face rather closer to the ceiling than her own and discovered that it was a handsome face and the man was smiling kindly at her.

"The non-fiction is depressing enough for me."

The man cocked his head to the side and gave her a searching look. She should have been embarrassed getting caught by a man as she wept into a sex position manual. But after spending an hour in stirrups today as a parade of doctors prodded her vagina, cervix, and uterus, the tattered remains of her dignity had packed its bags and headed west.

He coughed softly and Lela noticed he'd extended his hand. Quickly pulling herself together, she tucked the book under her arm and shook his hand.

"Brad."

"Lela. I'm a mess." She found his grip oddly comforting and didn't pull her fingers back from him.

"Are you going to tell me what's wrong or do I have to spend the rest of my life wondering why a beautiful woman was weeping over *101 Perfect Nights*? I mean, it's no *Kama*

Sutra, but it has a happy ending. Lots of them."

He meant the words as a joke but Lela couldn't laugh.

"No happy ending for me." She leaned tiredly against the bookcase.

Brad squeezed her hand a little tighter. She should have been scared of a man so big, built like a football player, dressed like a stock trader, and hanging out in the sex section of a bookstore. But something in his eyes made her trust him a little, and she needed to talk, had to talk. A stranger seemed better suited than a friend.

"No happy ending?" Brad crossed his arms over his broad chest. He had salt and pepper hair but looked no more than forty. "Every story should have a happy ending. Well, any story that has you in a bed in it."

"You're hitting on me." Lela smiled for the first time today.

"I'm flirting with you. I have the floggers back home when you want me to hit on you."

Lela raised an eyebrow at him. God, it would be nice to just spend a day in bed with a man like this—sexy, confident, and kinky too. But she knew it would end the way it always ended.

Pain. Tears. Apologies.

"I appreciate it. My ego needs all the help it can get. But I promise, I would be a waste of effort."

"I refuse to believe that, Lela. Tell me what's wrong. If you're not going to flirt back, the least you can do for *my* ego is to tell me why."

She wrinkled up her face in embarrassment.

"It's gross."

"Time of the month? Not gross. Easy to work around."

"If only. I..." she began and paused, deciding if she really wanted to be one of those people who told her life story to a stranger. Yes was the answer. Today. Yes. "I have severe endometriosis. I am twenty-seven years old and have been trying to have sex for ten years. Never had it without pain. And today the doctors—a whole team of them—stuck their fingers in me and said surgery was the only way to rectify things. Why have surgery to have good sex if I've never had good sex and don't even know if it's worth it?"

Brad brought her hand to his lips for a quick kiss.

"That is a sad story. So what's the book for?"

"This? They said I should try some different positions. I don't think they believed me when I told them I've tried them all."

"Anal?"

She nodded. "A couple times in college. Didn't go well."

"Did it hurt?"

"He didn't know what he was doing. Another fail."

"I don't know if this will convince you to stop crying into sex books and come back to my place with me but..."

"But what?" She let him pull her closer, close enough she could smell the cedar scent of his soap and see the smile that lurked at the corner of his lips.

"But...I know what I'm doing." He said the words with confidence bordering on arrogance and with such an intimate gleam in his eyes that Lela couldn't stem the tide of images his words conjured. The thought of a man inside her without her body seizing with pain?

"I've never gone to bed with a man I just met."

"No wonder you're crying in the bookstore."

"You won't think less of me?" She smiled at him.

"The only women I judge for their sexual choices are the women who turn me down. All none of them."

"I'd hate to break your streak."

"Then don't."

"It probably won't work, you know? I'm warning you right now."

"I'll probably have you screaming from pleasure in under an hour. I'm warning you right now. Say 'yes.'"

Lela laughed. Might as well. It was the least she could do for her poor vagina after all she'd put it through today.

"Yes."

"Good. Let's go."

"I have to buy this first. I got it wet."

"Trust me. Female tears are the least of the body fluids on this book." He took it and shoved it onto the shelf while Lela made a mental note to wash her hands thoroughly at Brad's place.

They grabbed a taxi and spent the twenty minute ride whispering abbreviated life stories to each other. Lela Moore, well-paid actuary, single, no kids, no hope. Brad Wolfe—he swore it was his real name—ex-wife, no kids, just a club he treated like his baby.

"What kind of club?"

"The best kind," he said and gave her a wolfish smile.

The club turned out to be exactly what she'd imagined. Black walls, ornate staircases, many rooms with closed doors.

"Sex club?" she asked as he escorted her inside.

"Kink club. We cater to all the fetishes here."

"Is 'terrified of sex' a fetish?"

"It's a damn shame, is what that is." Brad led her up the central staircase to a room at the end of a second floor hallway. He opened the door to a bedroom that appeared to have been lifted from a nineteenth-century house of ill repute. Seemed an appropriate setting for some behavior of ill repute. "Let's get you over that, shall we?"

"If you can do it, you're a miracle worker."

"I can do it if you'll let me. You've gotta trust me though." He opened an ebony cabinet inlaid with ivory and pulled out a flogger.

"Okay, you weren't kidding about the flogging thing?"

"I never kid about floggings. You say you're afraid of pain during sex. Fine. Let's get the pain out of the way first so you can focus on the sex."

"Are you-"

Brad strode to Lela and looked down at her. The move emphasized the height disparity. She wasn't short. Not at all. But he was so big she felt tiny in comparison and rather hated to admit how much she liked that.

"Lela...I know...what...I...am doing..." He said each word slowly and punctuated the sentence with a kiss. A long kiss, a slow kiss, a deep kiss that said even more than his words that he knew what he was doing.

"I believe you."

"Good. Take your clothes off."

She almost balked at the order before deciding she'd already come this far. What was stopping her? Off came her high heels, her skirt, blouse and bra.

"No panties?" Brad asked as she stood before him naked.

"I took them off at the doctor's office. Didn't put them back on again. I'm soaked with lube."

"A woman who comes pre-lubed? Love it."

Brad ran his hands up and down her arms. He touched her back, belly, and hips before cupping her breasts. He teased her nipples with his fingertips as he assaulted her mouth with the softest of kisses. The first stirrings of desire danced in her stomach. She'd been here before. The foreplay, the buildup, the hunger and need...and then wrenching pain and crushing disappointment. But maybe she could let go of her fears enough to at least enjoy the prelude to the disaster.

"Come here. Right here." He pulled her to the side of the bed and gave her one more kiss before pushing her onto her stomach. She tried to relax into the soft silk sheets as Brad adjusted the width of her feet still on the floor. She heard something like the clinking of metal and then felt something wrap around her ankles. Her legs were locked in, immobile.

"Brad?"

"Spreader bar."

"I can't move my legs."

"You're naked. Where were you planning on going?"

"Good point."

"Question. You said the last time you had anal was...?"

"College. Five years ago."

"I'm not small."

"I noticed."

"Stay here."

"Very funny," she said as she tried again to move her legs. She heard him rummaging through the cabinet and in seconds he'd returned to her.

"I need to open you up a little so I don't hurt going in. You still believe I know what I'm doing?"

"Yes. I think."

"Good enough." Brad dropped to his knees behind her, spread her cheeks open, and started to lick her.

"Wait..."

He pulled back.

"That 'wait' sounded like a 'wait, what the fuck are you doing' kind of 'wait.' I thought we already established-"

"Sorry. I just wasn't prepared for...you know."

"My tongue in your ass? Now you're prepared."

He started to lick her again and after a

minute she started to relax. Before her doctor's appointment this morning she'd shaved and groomed thoroughly. And if she could admit it to herself, it did feel weirdly good. Brad massaged her thighs while he kissed her and slipped a hand between her legs. He slid one finger into her vagina as he pushed his tongue inside her. A moan escaped her throat. The doctors told her to experiment with positions more. Maybe she'd call them tomorrow and tell them that she'd done her homework.

"Do fingers hurt?"

"No," she said, panting. "Fingers usually don't. Just-"

"Cocks?"

"Yeah."

"Please try not to sound depressed when I'm massaging your g-spot."

She laughed into the sheets. "Sorry about that."

Brad bit down hard on her right cheek and she gasped with the sudden pain.

"You have an amazing ass. That's not the only time I'm going to bite it today."

"Thanks for the warning," she said, still gasping.

"Another warning, I'm going to thoroughly lube you right now and insert a plug. It'll open you up."

"You don't ask permission to do things, I'm starting to notice. You just do them."

"Now you're catching on."

Brad started to ply her with the cold liquid, moving slowly inside her—one finger and eventually two. Before long she was started to feel something she hadn't quite expected—pleasure. Intense pleasure. His wet fingers deep in her...his free hand massaging her back, bottom, and thighs...his words of encouragement as she opened up to him...they set every nerve in the lower half of her body alight.

"Good girl..." Brad whispered as she moaned and dug her fingers into the sheets.

"Thought I was being bad here."

"Oh no. We don't play by those rules in this house. Any beautiful woman who spreads for me on a Monday morning? She's a very good girl."

Brad pulled his fingers out and Lela winced as he pushed the plug into her. It fit snugly but if she forced herself to relax, it didn't hurt at all. She felt a fullness from it, a pleasant penetration. She made a mental note to never try anal with a guy who didn't know what he was doing ever again.

She sensed Brad kneeling down again and unbuckling her from the spreader bar.

"I'm going to flog you. I have two very good reasons for doing that. My erection is just one of those two reasons."

He pushed his hips into her bottom and she felt the truth of his words against her skin.

"Do I get to know the other reason?"

"Endorphins. Intercourse causes you pain. Endorphins fight pain. I flog you and the endorphins start flooding your system. It's all very scientific."

"That's why we're doing it?"

"That and reason one." He pressed reason one into her hip again.

He turned her to face him and wrapped a silk scarf around her wrists. As he tied her wrists, she watched his face. He seemed utterly absorbed in the task and his dark eyes shone with intelligence mixed with desire. Without warning, she kissed him. He didn't object.

"I'm still going to flog you," he said when he pulled back from the kiss.

"I wasn't trying to stop you."

"I like you, Lela. I might have to fuck you all day."

"If you manage to pull this off without me in agony, I'll let you."

"Let me? Not sure I asked permission." He gave her a wink and spun her to the bedpost where he quickly tied her arms above her head.

Lela closed her eyes and took a deep breath, a breath that she released in a yelp as the flogger hit the center of her back. Brad took aim and hit her again. Up and down her entire back from her neck to her knees he flogged her. It hurt but not badly enough she needed him to stop. Every blow set her skin burning and her body flinching even as the plug inside her sent shivers of pleasure through her hips.

The flogging ended after a few minutes and Brad pushed his body into her back.

"I'd flog your beautiful body all day but my cock won't let me."

"A firm taskmaster, is he?"

"I try never to tell him 'no.'"

Brad untied her wrists from the bedpost and swept her up in his arms. The sudden removal of her feet from the floor set her laughing even as he laid her in the center of the bed.

"Don't laugh. I'm trying to be sexy."

"You are sexy, Brad." She gripped him by the back of his neck as he sucked her nipples one by one. "You don't have to try."

"Now tell me, what position do you most wish you could do without pain?"

"All of them," she said and he gave her a steely stare. "Okay. There's a version of missionary where her legs are up on his thighs. Always thought that looked so sexy spreading like that, ankles on opposite sides of the room."

"Nice. You can do that position in anal."

Brad sat up on his knees and unbuttoned his shirt. She watched him undress adoring every square inch of his thick, muscled body. He hadn't been kidding about the "big" part either, she noted as he rolled a condom onto his length.

"Knees to chest," he ordered and she complied. He worked the plug out of her and sat it on the bedside table. It shocked her how big it was. If that fit into her comfortably, so should he. Picking up the tube of lube again, he worked even more of it into her before slathering a generous amount over his cock.

He dried his hands, grabbed her thighs and yanked her close. Lela stared up at the ceiling as he positioned himself and started to push inside her. Inch by inch he worked his way in with slow, short thrusts. When her body gave him no resistance, he sunk deep and laid on top of her. As his hips settled between her thighs, her legs spread even further apart.

"Good?" He bit her neck.

"Very good," she breathed. Very good...she meant it. He was inside her, all of him, and moving, thrusting, fucking her. She couldn't believe that a man was inside her and she felt nothing but wanton pleasure. Brad put a hand to the side her head to hold himself up as he reached between their bodies and found her clitoris. With each slow deep thrust he rubbed the swollen knot. Her hips rocked into his. She couldn't get enough of his cock, his fingers, his mouth on her face, her neck. All these years, this is what she'd been missing.

Lela's body started to tighten. Her shoulders came off the bed and she buried her head against Brad's chest as her vagina clenched and her whole body shook with the climax she'd never experienced during sex before. Collapsing against the bed, she merely breathed as Brad pumped into her until his eyes shut tight and he came with a hoarse grunt.

Carefully he pulled out of her and laid on his back. Laughing, Lela crawled on top of him and stretched out across his chest.

"Verdict?" An arrogant grin decorated his lips.

"Verdict is...you totally know what you're doing."

Brad pulled her close for a kiss. The smile left his face.

"And?" She saw the question in his eyes.

"And...sex is amazing. I'm having the surgery."

"Good. Hurry up and schedule it so I can fuck your pussy in every position that's ever made you cry."

"That would be all of them."

"Then the sooner the better."

"How about now? My ass can take it."

"Now..." he said as he pulled her into lotus position and grabbed the lube again. "...would be perfect."

MOVIE NIGHT

The argument started the moment the movie ended.

"Not buying it," Leigh said, standing to stretch her legs.

"What aren't you buying?" Her husband Bryce caressed the back of her calf as she picked up the three empty glasses of wine and the bottle.

Ethan took the empty bottle and glasses from her and carried them to the bar. "You didn't like the movie? It's a classic thriller."

"It was a good movie," Leigh said. "Good acting. Good script. Huge gaping plot hole you could drive a dump truck through."

Ethan arched an eyebrow at her as he leaned back against the bar. Her husband's best friend since college, Ethan was a regular fixture in their lives. He'd been the best man in their wedding and had suffered good-naturedly through more than a dozen of her attempts to fix him up with friends of hers. She hated playing matchmaker, but any time one of her single friends got a look at the six-foot tall former professional soccer player, they all begged for an introduction.

"What's the huge gaping plot hole?" Bryce asked as his hand slid further up the back of her dress. She gave him a playful dirty look. Her black-haired, blue-eyed, too-handsome-for-his-own-good husband hit on her constantly when Ethan hung out with them, Bryce's not-so-subtle way of saying, *Look how fun being married is. Aren't you sad you're still single?*

Leigh swatted at his hand. "So the one guy convinces the other guy that they can swap wives in the night, right? 'Here, we'll sneak into each other's houses and while our wives are asleep, we'll initiate sex. And in the dark with them barely awake, they won't realize it's not their husbands fucking them.' That's the plot point, right?"

"What? We have sex all the time when one or both of us is barely awake," Bryce said, pulling Leigh down into his lap. "We did last night."

Ethan rolled his eyes, and Leigh winked at him.

"True," she said, remembering waking up with Bryce's erection pressing against her back. She'd pushed back against him, and he'd slid inside her. Without even exchanging a single word, they'd fucked for a few minutes before Bryce pulled out of her and fell back asleep. She'd followed him into dreamland only seconds later. "But I knew it was you obviously. If it had been some other man in the dark, I would have known. That's the plot hole. A woman would know if the man fucking her is or is not her husband even in the dark and half-asleep. That husband should have known he was getting played by his neighbor." Leigh got off her Bryce's lap. She took the DVD out of the player and turned off the television.

"You only say that because you know I'm the only man who's going to be fucking you in the middle of the night. If it was some other guy in our bed, and you were sleepy enough, you wouldn't be able to tell him from me."

"Oh, I could tell," Leigh said, crossing her arms over her chest. "Trust me."

"My cock *is* pretty amazing," Bryce said with a humble sigh. "I guess you're right."

"I think it could work," Ethan said, coming back to the sitting area holding a glass of wine. "You'd have to even the playing field though. No talking. Total darkness. Cock in pussy alone."

"He's got a point, babe. You know it's me because of my voice." He took Leigh by the wrist and pulled her back down onto his lap. "If you were blindfolded or something and two different guys fucked you without a word, you wouldn't be able to tell the difference."

"I could tell," she said. "And I can prove it."

"How?" Ethan asked, raising the wine glass to his lips.

"Just like Bryce said—blindfold me, don't make noise, and fuck me."

She looked at her husband who only laughed a little.

Ethan lowered the wine glass before he even took a drink of it. "You mean now?"

"Why not?" Bryce ran his hand from Leigh's ankle to her hip. "She dissed your favorite movie. You don't want to prove her wrong?"

"Dude, she's your wife."

"You didn't tell him?" Leigh asked.

"I thought he knew," Bryce said.

"Thought I knew what?" Ethan asked.

"Oh, we're kinky as fuck, Ethan," Leigh said.

"I knew he was. I didn't know you were," Ethan said to Leigh.

"We have threesomes at least once a month," Leigh explained as Bryce kissed her under her ear. "Usually, it's me and one of my girlfriends with him, but sometimes it's another guy. I'm never blindfolded though, and I always know who's fucking me. This could be interesting."

"Want to?" Bryce looked up at Ethan.

"Do I want to fuck your wife?" Ethan looked at Bryce and then back at her. "You don't even have to ask."

"I'll get the stuff," Leigh said, scrambling off Bryce's lap. "Are we in here or the bedroom? Preference, Ethan?"

He still wore a look of *Did I just win the lottery?*

"In here, I guess. I think I'd feel even

weirder doing this in your bedroom," Ethan said.

"Suit yourself," Leigh said and headed to the bedroom. She opened the trunk under the window and found the heaviest of their blindfolds. From the nightstand, she grabbed a box of condoms and the bottle of lubricant. In front of the mirror she paused long enough to tuck a stray tendril of red hair back into place and to adjust the straps of her pale yellow sundress she'd been running around in all day. Ethan always said he wouldn't get married until he found a red-head as sweet as her. Why should Bryce have all the luck? Leigh shimmied out of her panties and left them on the bedroom floor. Oh, Ethan. A wide grin spread across Leigh's face. Would he still think she was "sweet" after tonight?

She returned to the den where Bryce and Ethan had already moved the coffee table out of the way. Bryce laid a blanket on the floor over the Oriental rug. They'd learned the hard way not to fuck on that rug without something between her back and the rough pile.

"Put on some music," Bryce said to her. "It'll mask any stray sounds."

"I don't know if our speakers can get loud enough to mask your breathing, darling," Leigh said as she queued up some instrumental blues on her stereo.

"I get loud," Bryce said to Ethan who only laughed. "But I can keep it quiet tonight. It's just part of the challenge."

"Here. Take this." Leigh gave the blindfold to Ethan. "Can you tie it on me?"

"Yeah, of course. Are you sure about this?" he asked as she turned her back to him. He placed the blindfold, a thick black sash, over her eyes and tied it with a firm knot. The world went dark. She saw nothing at all, not even a sliver of light from above or below the blindfold.

"Bryce?" she asked.

"Go for it, babe."

Leigh reached behind her and found Ethan's hands. She pulled them around her body and placed them on her breasts. She heard Ethan's breath catch in his throat. With the blindfold covering her eyes, her other senses heightened, grew more acute. She felt Ethan's heart pounding as she pressed her back into his chest.

"Touch me anywhere," she whispered. "Bryce likes to watch."

She shivered as she felt Ethan's lips on her shoulder. He squeezed her breasts gently. The heat of his hands through the cotton caused her nipples to harden against his palms.

"Don't be nervous," she said as she took his right wrist in her hand and guided him lower. "I've wanted this with you for a long time. I even told Bryce."

"You did?" Ethan whispered back as he slid his hand under her dress.

She spread her legs and leaned back further into him. Ethan slid his hand between her thighs and carefully caressed her clitoris.

"I did," she said as she pushed her hips against his hand. "He's fucked a few of my friends. Only fair I get one of his."

"Only fair," Ethan agreed, pushing a finger into her. Leigh turned her head up and back and Ethan kissed her. Their mouths met, their tongues mingled, and all the while he fucked her with his finger. "You wouldn't believe how many times you've been in my fantasies." Ethan pushed a second finger into her wetness.

"Oh, I can believe it," she teased.

"Shall we?" Bryce's voice cut through the darkness and the haze of her desire.

"Definitely," she whispered against Ethan's lips.

She felt Bryce's hands on her waist as he guided her a few steps forward to the end of the blanket. Carefully, he brought her down to the floor. She stretched out on her back. Bryce gave her the tube of lubricant. She raised her dress to her waist and spread a thin layer of lube over her vulva.

"You both are just standing there watching me do this, aren't you?" she asked.

"Of course not," Bryce said.

"We totally are," Ethan said.

"Thought so." Leigh closed the bottle and sat it aside. Her heart raced in anticipation.

"We should make this game a little more interesting," Bryce said as Leigh opened her legs even wider.

"How so?" she asked.

"If Leigh can tell who's fucking her, she picks the next movie. If she guesses wrong, we do. For the next year."

"Sounds fair," Leigh said. "Hope you boys like old Hollywood musicals."

"I hate musicals, dude. We have *got* to win this game," Ethan said.

The room went silent but for the sound of the music playing in the background. Leigh strained her ears to hear any hints about what was happening in the room.

She sensed someone kneeling between her thighs and heard the metal jingling of a belt-buckle opening. Then she heard the foil of a condom package ripping. With each little sound she grew more and more aroused, more and more nervous. She really wanted to win this damn game.

The tip of a cock started to nudge against her vaginal lips. She reached down, spread her folds, and sighed as someone entered her in one smooth, slow stroke. The thrust was sure and steady. Must be Bryce then. Ethan would be more tentative as they'd never even kissed before tonight much less fucked.

Yes, she knew these thrusts...long, heavy, steady thrusts. Her husband's thrusts—loving, possessive...rough and tender at the same time. Usually by now, he'd have one of her breasts in his mouth and her clitoris between his fingers as he brought her to orgasm again and again. But the rules were already set— just penis in vagina and thrusting. She had to know the man by the feel and movement of his cock in her alone.

After a few minutes with the first man inside her, Leigh started to ache for an orgasm.

But instead, the man pulled out of her. She sensed him moving away from her.

"Want to take a guess?" came Bryce's voice. "Was that me or Ethan?"

"I think I need a comparison," she said. "Just to be sure I can tell the difference."

Bryce laughed, and she grinned at the ceiling and thanked God for giving her a husband as sexually adventurous as she was.

Once more she sensed a presence between her thighs, once more she heard pants opening, foil ripping. The floor creaked. Leigh sensed hands on either side of her shoulders. Again someone entered her—more carefully this time. She moaned at the pleasure of the penetration as either Ethan or Bryce, she didn't care who as long as he didn't stop, started slamming his hips into hers. She grabbed her legs behind the knees and held herself open wider. Bryce had fucked her like this many times—hard, fast, ramming into her like he'd die if he didn't fuck her into the ground in the next five minutes. But it could have been Ethan. He'd confessed just minutes ago that she'd been in many of his sexual fantasies. Perhaps this was him, his pent-up longing for her manifesting in this brutal pounding.

She gasped in surprise as she felt another presence right next to her.

"Can you tell yet?" came Bryce's breathless voice.

"Is it me or Bryce?" Ethan asked, his voice equally strained.

"Maybe she needs more to go on," Bryce said.

Leigh shivered as fingers slipped up her arm and pulled the strap of her sundress down her left arm and then her right. A few loosened buttons later and her bare breasts spilled out of her dress. A mouth, hot and hungry, latched onto her left nipple. But if that mouth belonged to the man inside her, she couldn't tell.

Another mouth found her right nipple and sucked it hard. She arched up off the floor as pleasure coursed from her breasts to a spot deep inside her hips. Still the cock inside worked her to a wet frenzy. She could feel her own fluid leaking out and onto the blanket beneath her.

A hand slid between her stomach and the male stomach above her. Two fingers found her swollen clitoris and teased it. The teasing turned to torture as those same fingers pinched and tugged it gently as the thrusts into turned from fast and frenzied to long, deep strokes that she felt all the way against her cervix.

"Who is it, babe?" Bryce taunted, his voice seeming to come from over her and next to her at the same time. "Who's fucking you right now?"

"You both are," she said knowing the cock inside her didn't belong to the fingers on her clitoris.

"Not quite..." her husband whispered. "But it's the best idea I've heard all night."

The man inside her, Ethan or Bryce, pulled out of her. Someone pushed her onto her side.

"You know what to do, Leigh," Bryce said, his voice quiet and commanding. She loved him most in his dominant moods when he took control of her body and used it like his own personal sex-toy. She did know what to do. She and her husband had anal sex at least once a week. While lying on her side, she pulled her knee up and into her chest as Bryce worked his lube-covered fingers into her, opening her up enough to take him inside her.

As she lay in position, she heard movement, footsteps, and men changing position.

Did this mean it was Ethan who now spooned up against her and started to push into her ass? Or was it a trick and once more was it Bryce behind her? Inch by inch, whoever it was pushed into her as her body strained to accommodate him. Once inside her, the man wrapped an arm over her chest and rolled them both onto their backs. Hands grasped her breasts and pulled her nipples. Someone took her knees in his hands and shoved them wide. Again the kneeling and the penetration. Leigh shuddered as the second cock entered her, this time shoving itself deep into her vagina.

Mute with ecstasy, Leigh could only breathe as the two men worked in tandem, fucking her with hard but careful thrusts. She'd experienced double penetration before. Bryce often put a vibrator in her vagina while he fucked her ass, but never before had she had two men in her at the same time. She'd never felt so filled before, filled almost to bursting. She felt everything, every nerve fired, every muscle tightened and contracted and stretched to take them both.

Fingers found her clitoris again and teased it. She came hard, jerking in the arms that held her. But the men, neither of them, were done with her. They continued to thrust into her. Each thrust in left her gasping. Each time they pulled out, she moaned. Her hands grasped at the shoulders above her as the chest beneath her back rose and fell and rose again.

It was too much. Sensation overwhelmed her. She came a second time and the cry that escaped her lips sounded pained even to her. The man in her vagina pulled out. The man beneath her rolled her back onto her side and slid out of her as well.

She thought they'd finished with her but two hands grabbed her hips and brought her up onto her hands and knees. She heard more foil ripping and in seconds the cock entered her vagina again from behind. Limp from her two orgasms, Leigh could do nothing but take it as the cock slammed into her. Hands gathered her breasts and held them as the man inside her rode out his own orgasm with a few final brutal thrusts.

Once more she was moved. This time she was made to straddle someone's hips. She placed her hands on his chest to steady herself while his penis slid between her wet slit and pressed into her. The two hands on her hips ground her against the hips beneath her.

When she felt a presence standing before her, she raised her hands. She felt the smooth skin of a flat male stomach under her palms as the cock pushed between her lips.

It nudged her throat and she opened her mouth even wider to receive it. One hand cradled the back of her neck. Fingers brushed against her cheek. If her mouth hadn't been otherwise occupied, she would have smiled.

She rocked her hips harder against the man beneath her. His hands dug into her skin as he worked her on his cock until he pushed up and into her once before going still under her. The cock in her mouth pumped a few more times before she tasted semen, warm and salty, inside her mouth. He pulled out and she swallowed.

Four hands put her onto her back. She tugged her dress up and buttoned the front. She smoothed her skirt down and rolled into a sitting position.

"I guess we win, Ethan," Bryce said.

Leigh reached up behind her head and untied the blindfold.

"It was you first Bryce," she said. "Then Ethan. Then Ethan again. You were in my ass, Bryce, while Ethan fucked my pussy. Bryce finished off while I was on my hands and knees. Ethan was under me while I was on top. It was your cock, my handsome husband, that was just in my mouth."

She raised her hand and wiped off her wet lips. Bryce and Ethan, both sitting side by side on the couch, looked at each other and then at her.

"If you knew, why didn't you guess," Bryce said.

"I didn't want to win too soon." She grinned at them both. "Then you might have stopped."

"How did you know?" Bryce asked.

"I knew it was you the first time," Leigh said, "because I could smell your soap. I buy the soap, so of course I knew it was you. When you were in my mouth, I could feel your wedding ring when you touched my face. The rest were educated guesses. Was I right?"

Ethan nodded. " guess we're stuck watching fucking musicals for the next year," he sighed, then smiled at Bryce.

He dropped his head back. "I hate musicals."

"Well, how about this idea..." Leigh said, crawling across the floor and rested her head in Bryce's lap. She reached out and took Ethan's hand in hers.

"What?" Bryce prompted.

She looked up at her husband and smiled. "Next time we have movie night, we just skip the movie."

THE CHAMBERMAID

The Interview

"**M**r. Edge explained the position to you?" Mr. Jonathan Rainer asked.

Cunt on command, Mr. Edge had said. *If you're interested, he pays better than I do. In six months, you can put a down payment on a pre-war in Brooklyn. He's too busy for girlfriends and likes his routine. Cold fish in my opinion, but maybe he'll surprise you. Interested?*

She was. She replied to Mr. Rainer, "In detail."

"You have questions?" he asked.

Are you a cold fish? she wanted to ask but didn't. He might be, hiring a girl for sex in such a cool, businesslike manner. They weren't even in the living room, but conducting this interview but his private office, which looked like it belonged in a museum, not a home.

Still, he was handsome. About forty, salt and pepper hair, more pepper than salt. Tall. Broad-shouldered in his Armani or whatever the stupidly rich wore these days? Neat beard and dark eyes that made him look like he'd stepped out of a painting by an old Dutch master. She was twenty-six, pretty but not stunning, and lived with two roommates. She wore vintage crochet dresses from thrift shops, and her long brown hair parted down the middle—not a hipster but a hippie, forty years too late. In her five years working for Kingsley Edge, she'd been a cocktail waitress, a stripper, a pro-submissive, and an occasional escort. They'd make an odd pairing, except who would ever see them together if her only role was to sleep with him every night?

"Will you hurt me?"

"Can you survive a spanking?"

"I have. I can." Spanking? She didn't expect that from him. Maybe not a cold fish, after all.

"I do, occasionally, like to share."

Ah, well, she knew it wouldn't be money for nothing. "I can survive that, too."

"I don't necessarily need you to enjoy any-thing. Just…allow it."

If the sex was halfway tolerable, it would beat cocktail waitressing by a long shot, Mr. Edge had said at the end of their conversation about Mr. Rainer's job offer.

Is he a good man? she'd asked him.

He'd shrugged. *We're not friends, just neigh-bors. And rich men don't go Heaven, remember, but he's not soulless. He takes excellent care of his employees.*

He was standing at the picture window behind his desk, looking at the city that made him. She didn't feel sorry for him—she never felt sorry for rich men—but she did sense a deep current of loneliness in him, more pro-found than he'd want to admit.

According to Mr. Rainer, these were the rules, privileges, and expectations.

Rules: If anyone asked, she was to say she worked for him as an assistant to the house-keeping staff. She was to be a chambermaid in all respects—taking care of his clothes, changing the sheets daily, tidying, cleaning, and picking up his dry cleaning.

Privileges: She would sleep in his bed every night in his home and have a room of her own for all her own things. His home was a townhouse on Riverside Drive, four stories, eight bedrooms, Victorian and masculine in decor. She'd expected minimalism or modernism, but realized after snooping online, the house looked the same as when he'd bought it five years earlier. Too busy to date and too busy to redecorate.

Expectations: From nine at night to nine in the morning, she was his, except for two nights a week off. Although if she gave him seven nights a week, she'd be paid overtime. Nights together, breakfast together, that was it. And she was to pour his coffee, naked preferably.

"Any other questions?" he asked.

"What will my first night be like?"

"I'll fuck you three to four times before I leave for breakfast. If," he said, "you'll allow it."

He turned to her and smiled, and she wondered if it would be the first and last smile she ever got from him.

Cassie said, "I'll allow it."

She got the job.

The First Night

CASSIE WAS MORE nervous than scared. She'd survived bad, awkward sex with men she barely knew before. She could do it again, especially in this beautiful bedroom, all hardwood and soft rugs, blue walls and ivory sheets, marble fireplace, and an oak fourposter bed.

The clock on the mantel softly struck nine. Cassie tensed as she heard the door to the sitting room open and close, then the door to the bedroom.

Mr. Jonathan Rainer stood in the bedroom doorway, his suit as impeccable as his timing. He looked at her. She was naked, sitting on the edge of the bed, waiting.

That pause, that look, revealed he hadn't expected her to be naked. He didn't seem to mind. He shut the door and came to her.

"Help me with my suit."

She rose and removed his jacket, hung it on the empty hanger in the walk-in closet. It smelled faintly of cedar, shaving cream, and smoke—a pleasant scent to her nose.

His eyes studied her as she returned to him. She unknotted his tie. He let her, but as soon as she'd pulled it free of his collar, he took her by the waist and stroked her lower back and hips. She smiled but otherwise ignored his touch, though his hands were large and solid and warm on her cool skin.

She unbuttoned his collar and then began on his shirt, but he stopped her and drew her over by the gas fireplace where a low fire burned to take the chill out of the spring air. He sat in the armchair and had her stand in front of him. Without a word, he wrapped his arms around her back, and his mouth closed around her right nipple. She stood stock-still, hands on his shoulders as he suckled her. His mouth was surprisingly hot, and her nipple hardened as his tongue brushed across the sensitive tip. She watched him sucking her—his eyes were closed, thick dark lashes resting on his cheeks, lips massaging the aureole. His beard lightly tickled her skin. He took his time—rolling his tongue around the nipple, circling it, sucking it, drawing it back into his mouth, deeper. He suckled her left breast, cupped them both in his warm palms, squeezed them firmly, possessively.

Cassie gasped softly when he pinched her nipples in unison, but he didn't let up. He licked and sucked her until her breasts felt heavy on her chest and her nipples throbbed.

Her feet went numb on the rug, but she found she didn't care.

Even when he finally pulled back from her breasts, he kept her standing in front of his chair.

"Spread your legs," he said, in the same tone he might have asked her to pass the salt.

She opened her thighs a few inches. With a surprisingly delicate touch, he pried open the folds of her vulva, lifted the little hood of her clitoris. She was waxed bare, so nothing was hidden. She was wet and swollen between her thighs. Arousal radiated from inside her, through her hips, into her stomach. She wanted to pump her hips into his touch but held back.

He seemed pleased by what he saw. She looked at him looking at her pussy, examining the wet red folds he opened. She sighed as he spread her wider. Her grip tightened on his shoulders as he dug two fingers into her vagina, up and in, deep enough to caress her cervix before pulling out.

"Bed." It was a command. Her legs quivered as she went immediately to the bed.

In anticipation, Cassie had already pulled back the covers. As he came to her, he shed his clothes quickly, without any fanfare even though he had a good muscular body worth showing off.

He slid onto the bed and knelt between her knees. On her back on the deep ivory sheets, she watched him stroking his cock. A livid red, thick, and dripping. She wanted it.

Without a word or even a kiss, he covered her body. He brought the head to the opening of her vagina and pushed it in. Then with his two hands bracing himself over her, he thrust into her, entering her fully with one deep stroke.

You don't need to enjoy it, he'd told her, *just allow it.* First, all she did was allow it. She lay back, breathing shallow breaths, allowing herself to be thoroughly pounded by his large stiff cock. Her breast still felt swollen and heavy on her chest. They bounced with each rough thrust into her.

She didn't want to just allow it, though. She didn't want it to be cold and businesslike between them every night until he got tired of her. To him, right now, she was nothing but a convenient warm body, a wet hole to be used, but she had her own desires.

Cassie stretched her arms over her head and took hold of the bottom of the head-board. She lifted her knees and dug her heels into the soft bedding. As he pumped into her, she lifted her hips, riding the entire length of him. His dark pubic hair grazed her throbbing clitoris. He moved his hips in a circle, and she gasped loudly. He looked at her, surprised but not displeased. He took her breasts into his hands again and squeezed them. He rode her hard but not brutally. She pumped her hips to meet his thrusts. Lusty sounds escaped her throat and filled the room, sounds that mingled with his soft grunts of pleasure.

Holding the headboard for leverage, she worked her slick cunt up and down his penis, bathing him in her desire. The sheets under them were damp with sweet and her fluids. She wanted him to come inside her, come in deep. She imagined thick white semen bursting from the tip into her womb, coating the clenching inner walls. The thought brought her to the edge of climax. The next pump of his thick organ into her sent her over the edge.

Her vaginal muscles clenched wildly at his cock, grasping it. He caught her ass in his big hands and impaled her as he came, driving his orgasm into her and bringing a cry out of her throat that surely the staff three stories down could hear.

When he was finished, he lay still on top of her. His heart was beating so hard against her chest, she couldn't tell his heartbeat from hers. He kissed her mouth, once but deeply. Their first kiss.

"Cassandra," he said.

"Jonathan."

He raised his head, looked at her. "I didn't say you call me that."

"You called me Cassandra."

"Did I?"

She nodded. "Yes. Jonathan."

He raised his head, glared. She almost laughed. "Your come is pouring out of me right now, and you're telling me I can't call you by your first name?"

She expected a barbed comment or a playful slap to the face or ass, like other dominant men she'd gone to bed with. Instead, he gazed down at her breasts, stroked them lightly, teasingly.

"Fair," he said. Then again, "Cassandra."

"Jonathan," she said again, for her pleasure only though it seemed to please him. His penis stiffened again between her wet thighs. He rose up and drew her to him, pulling her across his lap. He spanked her hard. After the first ten full-handed slaps she lost count.

When he stopped, her ass was hot and throbbing. He pulled her legs apart and worked three fingers into her sperm-slick passage. With a finger wet with his own semen, he worked his way into her ass.

Cassie had expected anal sex, but not necessarily on her first day on the job. Most men Jonathan's age would be done for the night or at least an hour. Not him. He took a butt plug and lube from his nightstand drawer.

"Can you take it?" he asked, showing her the plug. Big but not too big.

She said, "I'll allow it."

That remark earned her another spanking.

He lubed her thoroughly, taking his time, before working the plug into her. When it was in, he left her dangling over his lap as he massaged her ass and thighs, the plug inside opening her, stroking all the inner nerves. Then he pushed her onto her back on the bed again, mounted her, and worked his cock into her cunt. It was a tight, tight fit with the plug inside her, but delicious and after a few quick-fire thrusts, she came again, a sharp spasm of pleasure shooting through her body.

Now he did smile at her, a genuine smile. He turned her spent body over, put a pillow

under her hips and slowly worked the plug
out of her. As soon as it was out, his cock
took its place. He held her by the shoulders as
he fucked her ass with long, full strokes. Her
body opened to him. His penis was deeper
inside her than she'd ever felt. His fingers
clenched at her back as his thrusts grew
faster. It was its own sort of decadent pleasure to lay there and be used. She clutched
the sheets as he rode her, and when he filled
her again, she listened for her name on his
lips and wasn't disappointed. She repeated his
name, too, but silently, in her mind like a
prayer.

So it began.

The following nights were very much the
same. The mornings, too. This was their routine. She waited for him naked at nine. Soon,
like Pavlov's dog, her cunt would swell and
grow damp a few minutes before she heard
the door open and close at the same time
every night.

She'd wait naked. They would have sex
immediately, no delay. But this was only an
appetizer. After, he'd play with her body—
spanking her or tying her legs into obscene
positions. Almost every night, he fucked her
pussy and her ass. Then a bath around mid-

night. Had anything ever felt so wicked and luxurious as taking a bath in the middle of the night in a clawfoot tub, her cunt wrapped around his half-stiff cock for a slow leisurely fucking that never ended in orgasm, just back in bed, soft and warm and damp? She slept with him in his bed. Sometimes he'd roll on top of her in the night, fuck her half-asleep. She allowed it.

In the morning, he'd fuck her again. He liked her on top then, the curtains open to let the sunlight kiss her breasts and nipples. Breakfast was served. She was a good little chambermaid. She helped him dressed but remained naked to pour his coffee, and naked still, she would pressed her well-used body against his suit and straighten his tie one last time before he left her for the day.

At night at nine o'clock, it would begin again.

―――

An Important Conversation

A MONTH LATER, they were on the leather sofa in the sitting room that adjoined his bed-room. Saturday night—no work in the morning, a good night for lingering over their lovemaking. Jonathan had shed his suit jacket and tie, shirt open. Cassie was naked, straddling his legs. He dipped his fingers into a highball glass full of whiskey, dripping the whiskey onto her nipples, and lapped the liquid off. She was happy, and so was he, she could tell. They were comfortable together now, so she dared to ask him, "What do you do all day?"

"Work. Take meetings. Lunch at the club. Gym. Dinner at the club. I'm boring."

"A club? Like those old gentlemen's clubs in England? Rich white men with waiters in white gloves?"

"It's not all white men at my club. But the waiter does wear white gloves."

"Do you have drunken orgies there? I hope so."

"Sometimes though, I prefer sober orgies."

She'd expected him to say no, but he'd meant it. "You devil."

"I don't know why you'd be surprised. I have the sex drive of a lion."

The next day she looked this comment up —lions in mating season copulate dozens of times a day, up to fifty times.

To prove his point, he took his cock out of

his trousers and slide her down onto it. She settled in and moved her hips slowly. She wasn't done asking questions. Her cunt wrapped around his cock might make him more open to answering.

"How are you like this?"

He laid his head back on the sofa. "My father died of cancer when I was nine. Buried on a Saturday. Mom went back to work on a Monday. Someone had to pay the bills. I swore I'd never be poor after that." He ran his hands up and down her back. "I got married young but swore off kids until I was rich enough they'd never have worry about anything. All I did was work. Work, eat, fuck my wife, sleep, fuck my wife, work. One day I came home, and she'd packed her bags, told me if all I wanted was a girl to fuck, I should hire one. She was out. She got remarried six months later. They have three little girls. I'm happy for her."

He didn't sound happy.

"I'm sorry," Cassie said.

"Don't be. There's nothing good or beautiful about making the kind of money I make. I come home from it, and all I want is to feel something good. Good and honest. What feels better than an orgasm? What feels better than giving a beautiful girl an orgasm? Believe it or not, fucking you is the only thing I do all day that doesn't feel dirty."

She didn't know what to say, so all she said was, "Jonathan."

He met her eyes, smiled tiredly. "I've never fired a chambermaid. They all quit after a few months. No girl can keep up with me."

"What if you found one who could?"

"I'd fall in love with her and marry her."

"Sounds nice. I do like it here." Rich, handsome, incredible in bed, endlessly fascinating. She'd only scratched the surface of him. She grinned at him. "Test me."

He raised an eyebrow. His eyes glinted in the lamplight. "You really want to go down the path? You might not like it."

"I don't have to like it, remember?" she said as she brought her mouth to his. He drew her down onto his cock, to the hilt. Oh yes, whatever the test, it was worth passing. "But if you're there, I think I will."

―――

A Test Worth Passing

A SUNNY EVENING and Cassie had just returned from picking up Jonathan's suit at his tailor's when the phone in the bedroom rang.

Jonathan, of course. He told her a car would bring her to his club after dinner. He didn't tell her why.

From the outside, his club looked like any old uptown apartment building—pale stone facade, imposing, arched windows on the first floor, and a doorman who seemed to be expecting her. Inside it looked like the main floor of a once-luxurious hotel gone to seed. It smelled like cologne and cigar smoke. Only a few rogue beams of sunlight cracked through the closed red velvet curtains. Dust motes danced in the air. Stepping into the marbled foyer by the curving staircase up was like stepping a hundred years into the past.

A man walked out a set of grand wooden double doors. He looked about thirty-five, sleek brown hair, gray suit. If Jonathan stepped out of a Baroque painting, this man came off the cover of *GQ*.

"Cassie?" He said. "I'm Bret, a friend of Jack's."

Jack? Of course, that's what he called

Jonathan. Was she the only one who called him Jonathan? She hoped so.

She held out her hand to shake, but he kissed it instead.

"You're as beautiful as he said. Come with me." Bret led her up the stairs to a room on the third floor, marked with a brass #7 on the door.

Inside was a large bedroom, cold fireplace, and more red velvet curtains, more darkness. The bed frame was iron and had probably sat there for a century, too heavy to move. A remnant of a time when this city belonged solely to men like Jonathan and Bret, and no one dared question it.

The only modern touch was a laptop sitting open on the bedside table. Bret went to it, tapped keys. "Jack? You there?" he said.

Jonathan's face appeared on-screen. "Here."

Cassie moved in front of the camera. "Where are you?"

"Had an emergency meeting in L.A., but I wanted to see you."

She smiled. "See me what?"

Bret's hands found the small of her back. He stood behind her, close.

Jonathan raised his eyebrows. "What do you say?"

She glanced back at Bret, waiting for the verdict.

Cassie grinned at the camera. "I'll allow it."

Jonathan blew her a kiss. "Good girl."

A shiver passed through her body as Bret unzipped the back of her sundress. He pushed off her shoulders, and it puddled at her feet. She was acutely aware of Jonathan's gaze on her through the all-seeing eye of the camera as Bret took off her bra and slid down her panties. Bret kissed her shoulders, her neck. He took her breasts in his hands and molded them against his palms. Her nipples hardened. He turned her and sucked the red tips as Jonathan watched. Bret grinned at the laptop.

"Any requests?" Bret said.

Jonathan replied drily, "Several."

They did everything Jonathan ordered. Bret undressed, revealing a trim gym-toned body. She preferred Jonathan's thicker chest, thicker thighs, but Bret would definitely do for a night.

His penis was longer, not quite as thick, but with a large head. It was Jonathan's first request to watch her suck him. She went onto her knees and took the wet tip into her mouth, drew it in deeper. Bret tilted the screen to give Jonathan a better view of her mouth wrapped around the cock of a man she'd only met ten minutes before. It didn't feel like being with a stranger, though, not with Jonathan watching over the proceedings. She thought of him in a five-star hotel room on the West Coast, view of the ocean or Beverly Hills, sitting on a sofa with his cock in his hand, stroking himself off as he watched her fuck his friend.

He could have ordered up a girl from any L.A. escort service, but he hadn't. He'd wanted her, even 4,000 miles away.

Bret groaned as she licked the entire length of him. A delicious sound, she hoped Jonathan heard it.

Another order—put her on the bed so he could see her cunt. Bret moved the laptop, then pushed her in place, back onto the bed, cunt facing the camera. Bret spread her wide with his hands, let Jonathan see it all.

"She wet?" he asked.

Bret said, "Very."

"Fuck her."

Bret laid her onto her side and got behind her, lifted her leg, and worked his cock into her from behind. Classic porn position, letting the viewer see every inch of the cock fucking an open pussy. She was glad. She wanted Jonathan to see her taking his best friend's cock, wanted him to see she liked it, for him and for her. Her cunt took every inch. Her clitoris throbbed when Bret found it, stroked it. She moved her hips, wanted fucked deep.

"Good girl," Jonathan said again. In the little window on the laptop screen, she could watch herself, seeing what Jonathan saw, Bret's cock pumping into her from behind, her face flushed, ready to come. Her vagina was swollen and slick. Bret came out of her but only to push her flat on her back, mount her again. His cock speared her. She pumped her hips into Bret's, his hands gripping her breasts as he rode her, forgetting all about Jonathan watching from L.A.

Her orgasm built, and she came with a contraction that lifted her shoulders off the bed. As her vaginal muscles grip and released the organ inside her, Bret's head went back, and he cried out, pumping his come into her.

When it was done, she heard a strange sound. Applause.

She opened her eyes. Jonathan stood in the bathroom doorway, clapping.

"You bastard," she said, smiling.

Bret was already gathering his clothes. "I'll leave you two alone." He chucked her under the chin like they were old pals. Still naked, he walked out of the room.

Jonathan sat next to her on the bed. "I was supposed to go to L.A. I didn't want to."

"Why not?"

"Didn't want to go a night without you."

"Did I pass your test?"

"Not yet. One more."

"Ready," she said.

He laughed. Was it the first time she'd ever heard him laugh? "No, you aren't."

She rolled up and kissed him hot and hard on the mouth. He should have been in L.A. He didn't go because of her.

Again, she said, "Ready."

Jonathan lifted her off the bed and took her from the room to an ancient elevator at the end of the hall. It slowly descended, so slowly Jonathan had the time to push her up against the wall of the small compartment, take out his cock and lift her onto it. Pinned to the wall, Cassie shuddered as he gently fucked her sperm-slicked passage all the way to a shuddering stop.

The door opened. Jonathan carried her out. She felt weightless, languid, docile. She'd go wherever he took her. He took her into the room on the main floor behind the stately double doors. Men's voices spoke though she couldn't make out the words. The room was dark but for a scattering of brass lamps on, revealing the shadowy outlines of men in suits sitting or standing, heavy dark furniture, old and stately, and a long grand table where Jonathan carried her and laid her naked body on the end.

The man in the room gathered around her. How many? Four or five, she didn't want to count. It was like a dream, this sitting room filled with the scent of smoke and money, the men who ran the world surrounding her and Jonathan watching from the end of the table. A man, gray hair, about fifty, still handsome enough, got between her legs. She was pulled to the edge of the table. Between her thighs, the man's cock appeared, then disappeared into her. Hands of other men groped her breasts, even sucked them as she was quickly and roughly fucked. Her head fell back, and when she dared open her eyes again, another man—younger, taller, with a cruel smile—had taken his place. His cock was massive, the biggest she'd ever taken. She had to lift her legs to her chest and spread her thighs to take it all, but she did. Her body was supple, open, and slowly her vagina enveloped the enormous organ. Men on either side of her hips held her legs, watched the show. He grunted on her, spearing her to her core until he came with a shudder. Semen pooled on the table under her hips. Hot mouths sucked hard and hungrily at her nipples as they waited their turn at her cunt.

Not just her cunt. After the man with the cruel eyes pulled his limp cock out of her, she was turned over. Her ass was opened, and she felt at mouth licking lustily at the tighter hole. Fingers went in, spread it, and when she was open enough, she was penetrated again. She raised her head. A dark mirror revealed Bret was the man behind her, fucking her ass this time. She smiled as his fingers found her clitoris and worked it until she cried out like a whore. He laughed softly in her ear. They were like old friends now.

How many more men had her? Two after that? Three? She was taken to another room where a young man, not a day over twenty—

someone's virginal nephew or an intern, stripped naked and awkwardly mounted her. He rutted on her, his mouth clamped hard onto her nipple. Her inner muscles contracted suddenly around the cock pistoning into her, and the young man came with a shocked cry. Other men in the shadows laughed softly. She wasn't the only one being tested.

Her orgasms left her dazed, half-asleep. The men were like shadows over her. Only Jonathan remained in focus.

Late, very late, and Jonathan wrapped her in his long suit coat and carried her to a waiting car, Bret there to open the doors.

"You're a lucky man, Rainer," Bret said. "Where do I get my own chambermaid?"

"Call me. I know someone who makes excellent referrals."

The driver took them home, Cassie on Jonathan's lap, in his arms. He held her like a tired child and told her she'd been perfect, wonderful, everything he'd dreamed.

At the townhouse, he carried her up to the bedroom and sat her in his armchair. Under heavy-lidded eyes, she watched him perform her duties—pulling back the sheets, turning down the lights, taking off his suit. He came to her and dragged her to her feet, the coat falling to the floor as he lifted her out of it and impaled her sore and tender opening onto his cock. He put her on the bed and moved in her, kissing the taste of other men from her mouth. He licked her nipples, sucked the aching tips. She worked her hips under him. No matter how much she'd had, she would always want more of him.

"By morning, I'll be in love with you," he whispered.

She touched his face. She had won and smiled in victory.

"I'll allow it."

ABOUT THE AUTHOR

 Tiffany Reisz is the *USA Today* bestselling author of the Romance Writers of America RITA®-winning Original Sinners series.

Her erotic fantasy *The Red*—the first entry in the Godwicks series, self-published under the banner 8th Circle Press—was named an NPR Best Book of the Year and a Goodreads Best Romance of the Month.

Tiffany lives in Kentucky with her husband, author Andrew Shaffer, and their cats. The cats are not writers.

Subscribe to the Tiffany Reisz email newsletter to stay up-to-date with new releases:

www.tiffanyreisz.com/mailing-list

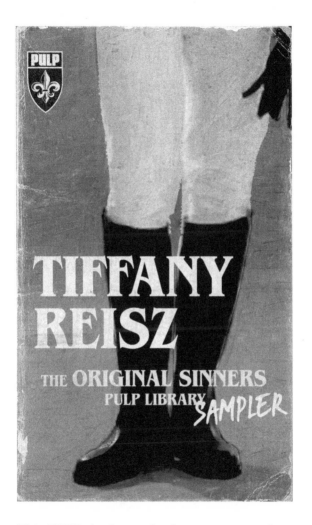

This **FREE** ebook sampler features excerpts from
seven Original Sinners Pulp Library titles. Down-
load at www.tiffanyreisz.com or wherever ebooks
are sold.